Acting Edition

I0591859

Ken Ludwig's A Comedy of Tenors

ıl SAMUEL FRENCH lı

MUSIC AND THIRD-PARTY MATERIALS USE NOTE

Licensees are solely responsible for obtaining formal written permission from copyright owners to use copyrighted music and/or other copyrighted third-party materials (e.g. artworks, logos) in the performance of this play and are strongly cautioned to do so. If no such permission is obtained by the licensee, then the licensee must use only original music and materials that the licensee owns and controls. Licensees are solely responsible and liable for clearances of all third-party copyrighted materials, including without limitation music, and shall indemnify the copyright owners of the play(s) and their licensing agent, Concord Theatricals Corp., against any costs, expenses, losses and liabilities arising from the use of such copyrighted third-party materials by licensees. For music, please contact the appropriate music licensing authority in your territory for the rights to any incidental music.

IMPORTANT BILLING AND CREDIT REQUIREMENTS

If you have obtained performance rights to this title, please refer to your licensing agreement for important billing and credit requirements.

KARAOKE TRACK REQUIREMENT

PLEASE NOTE: If you have obtained performance rights to this title, please visit concordtheatricals.com or contact your licensing representative to obtain the required karaoke music from *La Traviata* that is mentioned on page 34. This music has been provided by Musical Concepts (karaokeopera. com) and is available without any additional fee.

A COMEDY OF TENORS premiered in a co-production at the Cleveland Playhouse (Laura Kepley, Artistic Director; Kevin Moore, Managing Director) in Cleveland, Ohio in September 2015 and the McCarter Theatre (Emily Mann, Artistic Director; Timothy J. Shields, Managing Director) in Princeton, New Jersey in October 2015. The productions were directed by Stephen Wadsworth, with sets by Charlie Corcoran, costumes by William Ivey Long, lights by David Lander, sound by Joshua Horvath, and fight direction by Shad Ramsey. The Production Stage Manager for the Cleveland Playhouse production was Jennifer Collins. The McCarter production's Stage Manager was Alison Cote. The Assistant Stage Manager was Tom Humes for both productions. The cast was as follows:

SAUNDERS .... Ron Orbach

MAX .... Rob McClure

MARIA .... Antoinette LaVecchia

TITO.. Bradley Dean

MIMI... Kristen Martin

CARLO..................................... Bobby Conte Thornton

RACÓN... Lisa Brescia

CHARACTERS

SAUNDERS

MAX

MARIA

TITO

MIMI

CARLO

RACÓN

SETTING

The living room of an elegant hotel suite in Paris.

TIME

1936.

ACT ONE

Scene One

(We're in the living room of a hotel suite in 1936 in Paris. The hotel – the Faubourg Ritz – is part of Olympic Stadium, built for the Paris Olympics of 1924.)

(The room is light, bright and glamorous, as beautiful as any hotel suite in all of Paris.)

(There is a front door, center, opening onto a corridor. That is the only entrance or exit to the outside world. Two other doors, down right and down left, lead to offstage bedrooms. When the time comes, the bedroom downstage left will be for Maria and the bedroom downstage right will be for Racón. The room also has a balcony, stage left, that looks out onto the Eiffel Tower, as well as onto a soccer field one story below. There is also an outdoor patio, stage right.)

(The room also contains a sofa with an afghan over it, as well as some beautiful chairs and side tables. In front of the sofa and around the room are gift boxes beautifully wrapped, large and small, as well as several floral arrangements. These are the gifts that a visiting star is afforded by his hosts and fans when he comes to a foreign city to do a concert.)

(In the room, there is also a table with a variety of French catering on it.)

(Also in the room is a tin wash bucket with cleaning tools sticking out of it and a stack of folded towels. Clearly the maids didn't do a very good job of finishing their work.)

(The time is late afternoon on a beautiful fall day.)

(As the curtain rises, the room is empty and we hear an excerpt from Act Two of Puccini's La Bohème *– the section towards the end of Musetta's waltz where all the voices intertwine with passion – coming from a radio in the corner.)*

(After a beat, Henry Saunders hurries in through the front door. Saunders is in his early fifties and wears a business suit. He looks around the room, exasperated, then he turns off the radio and dials the telephone.)

(When the phone is answered, he speaks French with the misplaced bravado of a man who continues to believe the encouragement of his high school French teacher.)

SAUNDERS. *Bonjour. Je suis Henry Saunders. Oui, c'est moi. C'est vrai, c'est moi. C'est vrai. S'il vous plait, je veux parler avec Monsieur Max, le ténor. Merci.* I'll wait.

> *(He sees the wash bucket and picks it up with distaste; into phone.)*

Max! Get up here! I don't care if you're rehearsing, I need some help. The concert starts in three hours and Tito isn't here yet. And look at this place. Nothing's ready for him! There's all this food to put out, we need to check the bathrooms to make sure they're clean, you know the French, and oh my God, the maids have left some underwear on the floor.

> *(He picks up panties and hose from the floor and stuffs them into his pocket.)*

What kind of hotel is this?! Yes I know I chose it, but I shouldn't have to stuff underwear into... *Because I'm the producer! I was the Mayor of Cleveland! Now get the hell up here!*

(He slams the phone down and starts to clean up the room, talking to himself as he goes.)

The biggest concert in the history of opera, and I'm taking the cellophane off the cold cuts. What's this?

(He picks up something from the buffet table and it turns out to be a whole tongue; he juggles it with disgust.)

Ahhhh! It's a *tongue!* Uchh! Oh my God. What's the matter with these French? They'd eat the wax off the linoleum if it had vinaigrette on it.

(As he puts the tongue back on the table, there is a knock on the front door. Knock, knock, knock!)

Come in!

*(He pulls the door open and **MAX** enters, out of breath. **MAX** is in his mid-30s.)*

Max!

MAX. Mr. Saunders.

SAUNDERS. What took you so long?

MAX. No Tito yet?

SAUNDERS. Tito Merelli? Has he ever been on time in his life?

MAX. Sir, he is the most famous opera singer in the world.

SAUNDERS. And does that mean he gets to keep me waiting?

MAX. Well, sort of. Maybe his plane is late.

SAUNDERS. Well that would be a novel excuse. The last time he didn't show up was because of his drinking and womanizing.

MAX. Sir, I'm in rehearsal. You're paying an orchestra and it's downstairs waiting for me.

SAUNDERS. Max, I need some help up here! You were my assistant for *ten years*. Have you forgotten ten years of your life? Do you have amnesia or something?

MAX. No, sir. But now I'm an opera singer.

SAUNDERS. You're a what?

MAX. Oh no.

SAUNDERS. What are you again, Max? I must have missed it.

MAX. I'm a singer and you gave me a chance and-and now I have a career but we have a concert tonight in less than three hours and now I have to go back to rehearsal!

SAUNDERS. And I *want* you to go back to rehearsal, Max, as soon as you check all the *toilets* to make sure they aren't *filthy,* and make sure there's no more *underwear* lying on the floor, and *then find that jackass Tito Merelli!*

MAX. (*Picking up phone and clicking the clicker.*) I'm giving you three minutes, but that's *Ah, bonjour. Parlez-vous angl* – Oh, good. We're expecting Tito Merelli and his wife and they're arriving on –

SAUNDERS. Trans-America Flight 102 from Rome –

MAX. Trans-America Flight 102 from Rome, and we'd like to know if the plane is late. *Merci.*

> (*He hands* **SAUNDERS** *the phone.*)

Hold this. I'll check the rooms.

> (*He runs into one of the bedrooms.*)

SAUNDERS. (*calling to* **MAX**) Tito in Paris. Can you imagine? I'll bet he's out at the Follies Bergère, drinking champagne out of some filthy slipper.

MAX. (*offstage*) That's not fair!

SAUNDERS. Do you know what's riding on this concert, Max? My entire reputation's at stake!

MAX. (*offstage*) I know that, sir!

> (**MAX** *buzzes out of the bedroom, across the room, and into the other bedroom.*)

That one's fine. The bed looks nice.

SAUNDERS. That's all he needs – a good bed so he can have sex with the maid and sleep through the concert.

MAX. *(offstage)* You shouldn't give him such a hard time. He's been a really good friend to me, and I think he's going through a sort of personal crisis.

SAUNDERS. Oh, no. The poor thing. Is he off his linguini? Can't drink his chianti fast enough?

MAX. *(entering)* I think he's starting to feel his age. I mean, he's almost as old as

> *(stops himself)*

as some of the older opera singers who are still performing.

SAUNDERS. Really feeling your oats, aren't you, Max. Old man Saunders is heading over the hill, is that the idea?

MAX. No! No, no! I-I-I didn't mean –

SAUNDERS. I have fought to be in this position, Max. I've fought for thirty years, and now I'm producing the biggest concert in the history of Paris.

MAX. *(into the phone)* Hello? Yes I'm still here. Oh good! Thank you. *Merci.*

> *(hangs up)*

His plane landed a half hour ago, so he should be here any minute, now I have to go, they're all waiting for me.

> **(MAX** *runs out through the front door and is gone.)*

SAUNDERS. *(alone)* If I get through this week without a heart attack, it'll be a –...

> *(He spots something sticking out of the sofa. He pulls on it and it's a brassiere.)*

Oh for God's sake. Why don't they just put a sign up: "Welcome to France, Fornication in Progress."

> *(Knock, knock, knock! the front door)*

Max, would you stop horsing around! Just wait'll you see *this*.

> *(He opens the door and the Merellis are there.* **TITO** *is the famous Italian opera singer and* **MARIA** *is his stunning wife. They're dressed with style,*

*straight out of an Italian fashion magazine. They
both have strong Italian accents, and they both
look unhappy. They step into the room.* **SAUNDERS**
is still holding the brassiere.)

SAUNDERS. And with this symbol of the City of Paris, I bid
you welcome.

(He tosses it away.)

MARIA. *Ciao.*

TITO. *Ciao.*

SAUNDERS. How lovely to see you again. And how was your
flight? You had a good *voyàge*, I hope?

TITO. It was a-lousy, thank you.

SAUNDERS. Oh. I'm sorry. But I trust you checked in
downstairs all right?

TITO. That was a-worse.

MARIA. Tito, enough.

TITO. It was an insult.

MARIA. They didn't know.

TITO. They should have known! It's a-their job!

SAUNDERS. What happened?

MARIA. It was nothing. The girl at the desk, she thinks he's
another opera star named Carlo Nucci.

TITO. Carlo Nucci.

MARIA. She make a mistake. Is no big deal.

TITO. How could I be Nucci, eh? He's young, he's a-hot
stuff, he's the greatest tenor in the whole world!

MARIA. Tito, please.

TITO. I get in the taxi at the airport, on the radio is a-Carlo
Nucci. I get to the lobby, a beautiful girl with a big
a-chest, she say "*Bonjour,* Mr. Nucci, we are so proud to
have you in our hotel!"

MARIA. My husband is having a crisis.

TITO. Liar!

MARIA. Pig!

TITO. Witch!

MARIA. Child!

TITO. Diva!

MARIA. *Shut up!*

TITO. *Shut up a-youself!*

SAUNDERS. Well, you both seem to be in good spirits. Why don't I tell you about the logistics for the day, then we'll do the concert and ship you right back out. Ha! This hotel, as you can see, is part of Olympic Stadium where our concert will unfold in just three hours. *Tres horores.* Mr. Merelli, you know the running order, all quite standard, and soon *you*, your friend *Max*, and the famous tenor *Jussi Bjorling*, who arrived here yesterday from his home in Sweden – and who would have guessed

> *(with a Swedish accent)*

dey have der opera in a-Sveden but ja dey do – ha, ha! – the three of you will take the stage in front of thousands of your greatest fans for the concert of the century: *The Three Tenors!*

> *(Ring!)*

Excuse me. Hello? Yes, Jacques.

> *(covering the phone)*

It's Jacques Pessoir, my French assistant on the project. Cool as a cucumber.

> *(into the phone.)*

What? Jacques, calm down and say it slo – STOP STUTTERING!

> *(covering the phone)*

We don't think of the French as stutterers and yet –

> *(phone)*

What?! He *quit?! Jussi Bjorling just quit?! Don't move, I'll be right down! I will fix it, JACQUES, CALM DOWN BEFORE I STRANGLE YOU!*

(hangs up)

TITO. Is there a problem?

SAUNDERS. No. No, no. That was an exercise that Jacques and I do in case there ever *was* a problem, and he handled it brilliantly. But I think I should be going now to make sure that everything is running smoothly, the machine is in gear and *vroom* we're off!

　　　(He runs out.)

　　　*(**TITO** sits with his head in his hands and moans.)*

MARIA. Tito, what is a-with you?

TITO. I'm a-getting old, Maria. The stars a-fade. The lights a-go out.

MARIA. That's from *La Bohème.*

TITO. So what?! That's not the point! It used to be, the girls at the stage a-door, they were four a-deep. I sign autographs, they want to hug me. "Take a picture, Tito." "We love a-you, Tito." Now everybody want a-Carlo Nucci.

MARIA. Noo.

TITO. When I was young, maybe ten year old, I hear my own voice singing in a-church and it was so beautiful I say that's from a-God. I say thank you God, you are good man. After that, I sing everywhere, eh? Every opera house. Every concert. I'm a big a-star. But then, six month ago – I never tell you this before – I'm a-singing Donizetti and my voice a-crack on the high C. Just a-once, but everybody in the place, they look at me and go "Uh oh. He's a-getting old. It's a-good-bye Tito."

　　　(sob)

I cannot live this way without respect and honor.

MARIA. That's from *Madame Butterfly.*

TITO. Maria!

MARIA. Tito, you've got to stop this. You're in a-you prime.

TITO. My prime. Puh. I am being tortured in dungeon.

MARIA. That's from *Tosca.*

TITO. *Would you stop it!*

MARIA. But it's a-in a-you head! Your voice is just as good as ever! On the stage you got a-heart, you got a-soul! You still eat like a pig, but that's a-not new.

TITO. Pah.

MARIA. Hey. Nothing has changed! Except maybe you forget some things now and then.

TITO. I forget things? Me? Like what?

MARIA. It's a-not import. It makes no difference.

TITO. No! You tell me! I forget things. You tell me!

> *(She sighs.)*

MARIA. It's my birthday.

TITO. Today?

MARIA. Yeah.

TITO. Today is you birthday?

MARIA. Yeah.

TITO. Uh-oh.

MARIA. Yeah.

TITO. Hmm. I guess that explain why I'm carrying this a-bag around.

MARIA. Tito?

TITO. You're right, I forget a-so much.

MARIA. Oh, Tito! Look at this! You remember! Hoo hoo! I open now, yes?

TITO. No, you're gonna wait till next Thursday. Friday.

MARIA. You're very funny. You're like a-Bingo Crosby.

> *(She opens the box and finds a brightly-colored scarf.)*

Oh! It's a scarf! It's lovely, it's a-beautiful. Was it expensive?

TITO. Very.

MARIA. Excellent.

TITO. Hey. You want to celebrate? We got the bedroom, eh?

MARIA. Now? We just got here. We don't have our luggage yet.

TITO. You need luggage to make a-love?

MARIA. Well it might help. We got things in there.

TITO. Okay, fine, forget it.

MARIA. Hey, no. Don't be like this.

TITO. Like what? I'm a-fine. I gotta lay down anyway, take a nap. Us old people, we need to rest.

MARIA. Tito –

TITO. Hey, you want a younger man, you just gotta say so.

MARIA. Would you stop already! You are the best man I know, okay? And when our daughter get a husband, I hope he's just like you.

TITO. What has Mimi got to do with this?

MARIA. Nothing, I'm a-just sayin'.

TITO. Mimi get a husband in five year. Ten year. She's a baby.

MARIA. She's twenty-five years old.

TITO. Okay, *fifteen* year.

MARIA. She's a young woman. She's got a-urges.

TITO. Oh, sure. When she get to *puberty* you call me.

MARIA. Tito, she's past a-puberty. She's up to urges.

TITO. That's impossible! We sent her to boarding school in United States so she could be nice a-young girl and not get urges.

MARIA. Well she's got 'em, believe me.

TITO. How do you know this? Are you so smart?

MARIA. Because she talk to me. I'm her mother.

TITO. I'm not her father?

MARIA. 'Ats a-different.

TITO. What's a-different? My sister talk about urges with my Papa all the time.

MARIA. Your sister's only urge is to drive me crazy.

TITO. But she talk about it.

MARIA. That's not the kind of urge I'm a-talkin'! Women have needs, Tito. And sometimes more than you think.

TITO. More than *I* think? What, you got a man on the side for all the urges? Maybe you got two men. For urge a-one and urge a-two. 'Cause apparently I'm not doin' so good with number three!

MARIA. *Don't change the subject!*

TITO. *I'm a-not change!! The subject is Mimi, my daughter, my life, who is still a baby, and if any man even touch my girl, I'm gonna KILL HIM! And now I'm gonna take a NAP!!*

> (**TITO** *pulls the afghan off the sofa and walks into the master bedroom.* **MARIA** *follows him and they slam the door and they're gone.*)

> (*However…when the afghan comes off the sofa, it reveals their daughter* **MIMI** *in the arms of a young man. They're both wearing very little – just underwear and barely that – and they're both disheveled. Obviously, they were fooling around before* **SAUNDERS** *first entered the room, and they've been lying there frozen, under the afghan, ever since. As the afghan comes off, they spring to their feet, still standing on the sofa.*)

> (*Also, though* **MIMI** *is the Merellis' daughter, she was brought up in America and has an American accent, as does the* **YOUNG MAN**.)

YOUNG MAN. Oh my God. Your father's going to kill me.

MIMI. I know he is. I told you we should go to a hotel!

YOUNG MAN. This is a hotel!

MIMI. I meant a hotel that doesn't have my father in it!

> (*in the bedroom, offstage:*)

TITO. *I tell you Mimi is a good a-girl, she's the best a-girl, and she's gonna wait till she talk to her father!*

MARIA. *How do you know this?*

TITO. *Because if she doesn't, I'm gonna KILL HER!*

(back in the living room:)

MIMI. This comes perilously close to French farce.

YOUNG MAN. I think we should get out of here as quickly as possible.

MIMI. I think that's a very good idea.

> *(They spring into action. **MIMI** grabs a second afghan off the chair and pulls it around her, then they desperately look for their clothes.)*

YOUNG MAN. *Where are my pants? They were right here!*

MIMI. *Shh!*

YOUNG MAN. *Where are my pants?!*

MIMI. I'll tell you *after I find my dress!*

> *(At which moment, the door to the bedroom flies open and we see **MARIA** calling back into the room, holding the knob, but facing into the bedroom, calling to **TITO**. **MIMI** and the **YOUNG MAN** plaster themselves against the wall and freeze.)*

MARIA. I get a-you pills!

TITO. *(offstage)* I don't want a-pills! And where's a-the luggage?

MARIA. I'll call downstairs.

TITO. *(offstage) So do it already!*

MARIA. *Fine!*

TITO. *(offstage) FINE!*

> *(Bang! **MARIA** goes back into the bedroom and slams the door, never having seen the two kids.)*

YOUNG MAN. Did I just have a heart attack?

MIMI. Are you still breathing?

YOUNG MAN. Yes.

MIMI. Then no.

YOUNG MAN. Ha! There's my pants! Oh, thank God. Oh they're so beautiful!

> *(He starts pulling them on.)*

MIMI. Wait!

> *(She gazes romantically into the distance.)*

You know this does have something timeless about it. Two young lovers, defiant in the face of the old generation that would stand in the way of their innocent desires. It reminds me of *A Midsummer Night's Dream* without the fairies. Embrace me.

> *(They embrace.)*

My God, I love you.

YOUNG MAN. I love you too, but I'll love you more if we get the hell out of here.

MIMI. Right! Let's move!

YOUNG MAN. Wait! Don't you have a big audition or something?

MIMI. That's not till five. It's three o'clock.

YOUNG MAN. It's four-thirty.

MIMI. *(scornfully) It is not.*

> *(He shows her his watch.)*

Oh my God! Did we fall asleep?

YOUNG MAN. I think so.

MIMI. *Oh my God!* This is your fault.

YOUNG MAN. My fault?

MIMI. Yes! You're just like a man –

YOUNG MAN. I'm *like* a man –?

MIMI. You act all lovey-dovey till the chips are down, then you fall asleep, *now where's my dress?!*

YOUNG MAN. *Well I can look for it if I get my pants on first!*

> *(He's hopping around on one leg, struggling to get his trousers up – at which moment, **MARIA** re-enters.)*

MARIA. *(calling back to **TITO** and closing the door behind her)* I think I left my purse in the –

(She sees the two kids frozen in place and gasps. The kids gape at her – then **MIMI** *falls to her knees and holds her hands up in prayer.)*

MARIA. Your father's gonna kill you.

MIMI. Yeah, I know. Help us? Please?

YOUNG MAN. I'm really sorry about this.

*(***MARIA*** *hisses at him like an angry cat.)*

MIMI. Mom listen, I'll explain everything later, but I think my dress must be in there, and I have an audition in twenty minutes. They're shooting a movie here in Paris about the French Revolution and they want to see me.

MARIA. A movie?

MIMI. I play a French peasant girl who confronts the Queen of France and begs for food. It's a small part, but I do have one really good scene and I get to cry in it.

MARIA. That's important?

MIMI. I could get noticed.

MARIA. We gotta move.

TITO. *(offstage)* Hey, Maria, my back's a-killin' me. Could you give me a rub? It's my left a-shoulder.

MARIA. The angels are weeping, I'm a-*coming!*

(to the kids, whispering)

Stay here. I get you clothes. And be *quiet.*

MIMI. Thanks, Mom. I love you. It's a dress and shoes. Hurry up!

*(***TITO*** *starts opening the door, trying to get into the living room, but* **MARIA** *holds the door shut.)*

MARIA. No!

TITO. *(offstage)* Hey, you said a-you rub my back.

MARIA. Back! Stay back!

TITO. Maria, what's a-matter?

MARIA. *Nothing's the matter, just a-stay in you bed!*

(As **TITO** *tries to get into the living room,* **MIMI** *panics. She runs to the balcony, but the*

> YOUNG MAN *is holding one end of her afghan: so*
> *as she runs, she spins out of the afghan, reaches*
> *the balcony and flies off it with a cry of surprise.*
> MARIA *and the* YOUNG MAN *gasp in shock.)*

> *(Enter* TITO, *hitting the* YOUNG MAN *in the head*
> *with the door while hiding him behind it. From*
> TITO*'s perspective, the room is empty.)*

TITO. It feels like a-somethin' funny's goin' on. Holy cow!

MARIA. What?!

TITO. There's a naked girl running across the Stadium. Look!

> *(*MARIA *looks and is immensely relieved.)*

MARIA. Whoo. Yah. She's naked okay.

TITO. *(peering)* She look familiar.

MARIA. *(Pulling him away.)* Ya, sure, it's a-Eleanor Roosevelt, now get in you bed!

> *(The connecting door starts swinging closed*
> *revealing the* YOUNG MAN *standing behind it.*
> *He's holding his head, swaying from the bang of*
> *the door.* MARIA *sees him and panics and slams*
> *the door against the wall to hide him again. We*
> *hear it hit his head again with another bang.)*

TITO. Okay, okay!

> *(*TITO *can tell that something isn't right – but*
> MARIA *pushes* TITO *through the door, into the*
> *bedroom, and slams it shut.)*

YOUNG MAN. *(whispering)* Mrs. Merelli –

MARIA. No, stop. Mimi has told me all about you and I forgive you. How's a-you head?

YOUNG MAN. It hurts.

MARIA. Take this scarf and press.

> *(She hands him her new scarf and he presses it*
> *against his head.)*

YOUNG MAN. *Ow!*

*(At this moment, **TITO** opens the door a crack and listens in the doorway. **MARIA** and the **YOUNG MAN** don't see him but the audience sees him clearly.)*

MARIA. Now get a-you clothes on quick before my husband see anything.

YOUNG MAN. *I'm trying!*

MARIA. *Shh!* Keep a-you voice down. If my husband knew about this, he would *kill* you!

*(**TITO**'s mouth drops open.)*

TITO. *(to himself)* Maria!

YOUNG MAN. *(as he pulls his pants up)* I want you to know that I wasn't just fooling around in here. It wasn't just sex. We're in love. We're *both* in love.

TITO. *(to himself)* Oh my God.

MARIA. Of course it is love. It is what I have wished for. You are the perfect man.

TITO. *(to himself)* Maria is having an affair!

MARIA. You are young. You are vital. You have muscle like bull.

YOUNG MAN. Hey, you're not so bad yourself.

TITO. *(to himself)* Maria!

MARIA. How's a-you zipper?

YOUNG MAN. I think I've got it.

(Pulling it up with difficulty.)

Unh!

*(**MARIA** kneels and tries to help him with the zipper. **TITO** looks around the door and sees his wife kneeling in front of the **YOUNG MAN** and thinks the worst. He recoils in shock.)*

MARIA. I tell you, this thing, it make a-me happy. The way a woman is happy. From deep inside.

YOUNG MAN. But listen. We've got to tell your husband, soon. We have to be honest about this.

MARIA. Hey, let me decide, okay? I know how to break it to him.

YOUNG MAN. If you say so.

TITO. *(to himself)* Look at him! He's a-twenty years old!

> *(Without thinking about it, the* **YOUNG MAN** *puts* **MARIA***'s scarf into his breast pocket.)*

TITO. Hey thanks for everything. You're fantastic.

MARIA. You're not so bad a-youself, you know. Ha!

YOUNG MAN. *Ciao.*

MARIA. *Ciao.*

> *(The boy gives* **MARIA** *a kiss on the cheek and hurries out the front door.* **MARIA** *sighs with happiness.* **MIMI** *has found a wonderful boy.)*

> *(Meanwhile,* **TITO** *totters back into the bedroom and we hear the first five chords of Puccini's* Tosca *– a passage of monumental despair.)*

MARIA. *(turning to the door)* Okay, roll over. I fix a-you back.

> *(***MARIA** *cracks her knuckles, enters the bedroom and closes the door; at which moment,* **SAUNDERS** *and* **MAX** *enter from the hall.* **SAUNDERS** *is on the rampage.)*

SAUNDERS. *I don't believe it, how could this happen?!*

MAX. Well under the contract, sir, it's not prohibited.

SAUNDERS. Oh, please. Do you mean to say that less than *three hours* before the concert, Jussi Björling, the Swedish songbird son of a bitch, can simply walk out the door whenever he *pleases?!*

MAX. Well that's not exactly how I'd –

SAUNDERS. *I will sue the bastard for his next herring allotment!*

MAX. Sir –

SAUNDERS. He'll sing his next *Don Carlo* in his *underwear* at the *Stockholm Light Opera and Storm Door Company!*

MAX. Sir, his mother died!

SAUNDERS. "His mother died"? Excuse me. Am I missing something? Doesn't everybody die, Max? Mothers die every day of the week! Whup, it's three o'clock. There goes mom. Whup, it's three-oh-one, now grandma's gone. Does this surprise you, Max?

MAX. He said he was sorry. He knew it would cause inconvenience.

SAUNDERS. "Inconvenience?" Is that what this is, Max?

MAX. No, no, I understa –

SAUNDERS. Oh my goodness, we've had a little inconvenience.

MAX. Sir, he's in mourning.

SAUNDERS. *(dialing)* Well he must be! He's gone back to his Viking ancestors to set fire to his mother's boat! Jacques listen to me, we have to change the advertising. Call it "The Two Tenors." *Les Deur Tenores...* No, Mr. Björling is not coming back! Apparently he's a mama's boy... Well he's Swedish, Jacques. Courage is not their hallmark, now is it? Now I want you to call every agent in Paris and see if by some miracle we can find a replacement for the Coward of Copenhagen.

MAX. That's Denmark, sir –

SAUNDERS. Yes that's right, Jacques. We have two hours and forty minutes. You have mastered the watch-face at last. We're looking for a singer, preferably a tenor, preferably living, but I'll take a baritone, a bass or *a dead soprano just get somebody the hell up here!!*

(*He slams down the phone.*)

MAX. I bet you'll find somebody in time, sir.

SAUNDERS. How optimistic of you. Is this the same spirit in which you impregnated my only daughter?

MAX. Sir, she's my wife!

SAUNDERS. Don't remind me, Max!

MAX. *(in the same tone)* Sorry, Henry!

SAUNDERS. And now my little Maggie is back in Cleveland waddling around like a duck because you couldn't control yourself. Max, listen to me. You keep Maggie safe, you keep her happy, you treat her like a queen. That is the secret to a good marriage. I know. I've done it four times.

> (*Ring!*)

Yes?! What is it, Jacques? Stop stuttering and say it slo –!

> (*He listens and his face lights up. Something wonderful has happened.*)

You're kidding. Honestly? Ha ha! Just like *that?!* That's fantastic! Yes of course I'll meet with him! I'll be right down!

> (*He hangs up.*)

MAX. What happened?

SAUNDERS. Ha ha! Hahahahaha! Thank you Gods of Commerce!

MAX. What?

SAUNDERS. We've got a lead on a third tenor. First call he made, like *that*. I love that boy. Now you stay here in case *Il Stupendo Alcoholico* has a sudden urge for his favorite chianti.

MAX. But my rehearsal –

SAUNDERS. Forget your rehearsal! I want Tito alive, sober and in his tuxedo by six o'clock or I'm firing you, now stay right here!

> (**SAUNDERS** *rushes off, slamming the door behind him, at which point* **MAX** *hears an argument in the bedroom:*)

MARIA. (*offstage*) Tito, what is the matter with you? Are you sick?!

TITO. (*offstage*) Oh yeah I'm a-sick all right.

MARIA. (*offstage*) But you want a-my back rub!

TITO. (*offstage*) I want a-you nothing! Just leave me alone!

> (*Bang!* **MARIA** *enters, striding for the front door, with* **TITO** *behind her. They're having a full-scale argument.*)

MARIA. *Okay! You want alone, I leave alone!*

TITO. *That's a-fine with me!*

MARIA. For twenty-five years I gotta put up with this life. I'm not a-Maria anymore, I'm *a-Mrs. Tito!* "Excuse me, Mrs. Tito, I gotta push you into the *soup* 'cause maybe you husband's gonna smile at me and *I'll have a religious experience on a-you carpet.*"

TITO. *Gypsy!*

MARIA. *Pig!*

TITO. *Maniac!*

MARIA. *Tenor!*

> *(Bang!* **MARIA** *exits through the front door, slamming it behind her.)*

MAX. *(false good spirits)* Hey! Tito!

TITO. *(distraught)* Max! It's a-good to see you.

MAX. It's good to see *you.*

> *(They embrace and* **TITO** *holds* **MAX** *tightly.)*

TITO. You are my *friend,* Max. It's a-good to have friends.

MAX. Hey, what's the matter?

TITO. It's a-nothing. It's just a-marriage, I guess. It's just –

> *(He starts to cry.)*

MAX. Tito, what happened?!

TITO. Maria. She is unfaithful to me.

MAX. Maria? Nooo.

TITO. Yes.

MAX. It's impossible.

TITO. It's a-true.

MAX. I don't believe it for a –

TITO. *(grabbing* **MAX** *by the shirt-front and shaking him)* Maria *is unfaithful to me!!*

MAX. Tito, *Tito!* How do you know?

TITO. Because I saw them!

MAX. *You saw them?!*

(**TITO** *nods.*)

MAX. You actually saw them –?

(*He puts his palms together.*)

TITO. No, more like a –

(*with his two index fingers he indicates what he saw through the door*)

MAX. Then you didn't see them –?

(*swimming palms*)

TITO. Not exactly, but I *watched* them. They were talking about their big a-love, their big a-muscle. He's young, he's a-vital. She said his thing make her happy!

MAX. Oh my God.

TITO. Oh, Max, I can't believe it! After all these years, we work a-so hard at this life together. But now it's like a darkness come inside me. Is like a nightmare.

MAX. Look, look, I-I-I just don't believe it, okay? I think you must have misunderstood something.

TITO. Never!

MAX. Oh, come on! Of course you did. I mean maybe, *maybe* she flirted with someone, I'm not saying she did, but you know how it is, we all do it now and then, it's natural. I'll bet you've done the same thing, right? But you never got serious with another woman.

TITO. I did once.

MAX. You did?

TITO. Before Maria and I were married.

MAX. *Before?* That's hardly an affair, you know.

TITO. But it was crazy because I loved Maria.

MAX. What happened?

TITO. I got a-swept away. It was the famous soprano, the great Racón.

MAX. Tatiana Racón?

TITO. Tatiana Racón.

MAX. Holy cow, she's incredible. She's in Paris this week doing Salomé at the Garnier.

TITO. She is a-from Russia. Racón. She was gentle and had a-such deep emotion, she could be laughing and a-crying at the same time. We had a-one night here in Paris while Maria was waiting for me in Vienna. I was unfaithful, now she is unfaithful. I have sealed myself in my own a-tomb.

MAX. That's from *Aida*.

TITO. That's not the point!

SAUNDERS. *(offstage)* Max!

MAX. That's Mr. Saunders. Now just remember: Maria did nothing wrong.

SAUNDERS. *(entering in high spirits)* Max! Wait till you hear this! Ha haaa! Hello, Tito. And how's your wife? Out getting her claws sharpened? Ha! Now guess what happened?

MAX. I don't know, but it sounds like good news.

SAUNDERS. Good? I think you could say that.

MAX. Did we get Jussi back?

TITO. Jussi left?

MAX. I thought so.

SAUNDERS. No, we didn't get Jussi back. Who needs the bastard? We've upped the game, the stakes are high and we're flying with the big boys! Do you know, in a way, I sort of owe one to Jussi Bjorling. Let's send him flowers. It *was* his mother, you know.

MAX. Sir –

SAUNDERS. Now *guess* who is singing with you and Tito at the concert tonight.

MAX. Uh, Lauritz Melchior?

SAUNDERS. Nope.

TITO. Beniamino Gigli?

SAUNDERS. Better. Younger.

MAX. Younger? Oh my God, it isn't –?

SAUNDERS. Oh yes it is. It's *Carlo Nucci!!*

TITO. Agh!

SAUNDERS. And here he is!

> (SAUNDERS *opens the door and there is the* YOUNG MAN *we met earlier who is Mimi's lover. He is* CARLO NUCCI. TITO *lets out a cry and springs at* CARLO *and starts to strangle him.* MAX *and* SAUNDERS *try to stop him.)*

> (*During the strangling, we hear the final, super-charged moments of the trio "Cedo al destin orrible" from Act Two of* Il Pirata *by Vincenzo Bellini.*)

> (*Blackout.*)

Scene Two

(Two minutes later. **TITO** *and* **MAX** *are alone in the living room.* **MAX** *is calling into the bedroom, right.)*

MAX. We'll be right with you, sir. Carlo. Just a minute.

(He closes the door. The following goes quickly.)

TITO. I tell you, it was him!

MAX. Tito –

TITO. I'm not a-crazy!

MAX. But you could be mistaken.

TITO. No!

MAX. You saw him –

(index fingers)

TITO. Yah.

MAX. But not –?

(palms)

TITO. That's enough! Max. Oh, Max, it was like a nightmare! And she give him the scarf I gave her this morning for her birthday, which I chose a-myself! It was like she gave him my heart, my lung, my kidney.

MAX. You're sure about this?

TITO. *I was watching!*

MAX. And where did this happen?

TITO. Right here in this room.

MAX. And where were you?

TITO. In there!

MAX. You saw him through the door?

TITO. Yah.

MAX. And where were you just before that?

TITO. I was at the balcony, watching the naked girl run across the field.

MAX. There was a naked girl on the field?

TITO. Yah.

MAX. Did you recognize her?

TITO. Yah. She look a-something like my daughter Mimi. Or Mrs. Roosevelt.

MAX. And where were you before the naked girl episode?

TITO. On the bed.

MAX. Asleep?

TITO. Yah.

MAX. Tito, you were having a dream.

TITO. No.

MAX. Yes! Just think about it. You're worried about Mimi getting married, right? You and Maria have an argument, you lie down and you fall asleep. Then you have this *dream* where you see a naked woman who looks like your daughter. Then you see your wife through a door having an affair with a guy who's twenty years younger than you, and then *he* turns out to be your biggest rival! Tito, it was a dream! It had to be!

TITO. Impossible.

> (**MAX** *picks up a pad of paper and sits in the chair next to the sofa, as* **TITO** *reclines on the sofa. So they are now in the classic pose of psychiatrist and patient.*)

MAX. Look, I took this course in *psychology* in college. It's a whole new field. You've heard of Sigmund Freud? He wrote this book called

> (*Writing on the pad and tearing the sheet off and handing it to* **TITO**.)

The Interpretation of Dreams, and believe me, a naked girl running across a soccer field while your wife is helping your biggest rival get dressed through an invisible door? – you'll be in the sequel if you're not locked up first.

TITO. But it seem so real and had all the things that keep me up at night. Singing. Women. Age. Sex. My daughter. Women.

MAX. You owe Carlo an apology, you know. And can I be honest? For me this concert is a really big deal. I mean I know I'll never sing like you, but I could have a good career, and this concert would take things to a whole new level. And with the baby coming –

TITO. How is Maggie?

MAX. She's due next week. And here *I* am, being an "artist" while she's –…

TITO. I know this feeling.

MAX. Yeah.

TITO. Okay. I do it for you. We do the concert.

MAX. Really? All right! Thanks, Tito. You're the best. Let's tell 'em.

> (**MAX** *calls into the guest bedroom.*)

Okay, gentlemen. Come on in.

> (**SAUNDERS** *and* **CARLO** *enter the living room.*)

SAUNDERS. Well?

TITO. I make a-mistake.

CARLO. *(rubbing his neck)* You sure did.

TITO. I'm a-sorry. Here's a-my hand.

> (**TITO** *and* **CARLO** *shake hands.*)

CARLO. Oh good. Wow. I'm so glad. I mean, I could understand if you…

TITO. No no. You are good singer. You have beautiful voice.

CARLO. But not like yours.

TITO. No.

CARLO. You're my idol. I've always wanted to meet you, my whole life.

TITO. No –

CARLO. I swear to God. I was raised in Brooklyn – my parents are Italian – and all my father ever talked about was Tito Merelli. On the radio we heard you in *La Traviata* and oh my God, we sat there with tears in our eyes. You're the best there is.

TITO. Perhaps I misjudged you.

SAUNDERS. You know, we're doing *Traviata* in the concert tonight.

CARLO. The Libiamo?

TITO. Of course.

MAX. Hey, wait a second. Let's rehearse it.

CARLO. Now?

MAX. Why not? We're all here. And we need to assign the lines anyway.

CARLO. It's all right with me.

TITO. *Si si, proviamo.*

MAX. Great! That's great! Now you stand here. Good.

> *(The three singers face the audience.)*

Now we've got to imagine that out there – no this way – right out there is a big audience. Thousands of people! And-and they've come here just to hear us sing. So, okay, the announcer goes to the microphone and looks out at the crowd:

> *(**MAX** picks ups the telephone receiver and uses one end of it as if it's a microphone.)*

"*Mesdames et Messieurs: C'est un plaisir de vous prèsenter Les Trois Ténors!* – I took French in college – *S'il vous plait, applaudissez…*

> *(into the phone)*

Oh, sorry, I was…

> *(He hangs up the phone.)*

applaudissez pour MAX, LE TÉNOR!

> *("Whooooooo!" – he imitates the sound of an audience responding – and he bows.)*

Et le ténor célèbre CARLO NUCCI!

> *("Whooooooo!" – and **CARLO** salutes.)*

Et finalement, le plus grand star de la firmament, le grand chanteur, TITO MERELLI!!

("Whoooooooooooo!" – **TITO** *gives a flourish.)*

MAX. Okay, like Tito always tells me, we've gotta hear the music. It's in our heads. Shh. Listen.

(They listen hard.)

(silence)

(And then the music begins. It's the lively introduction to the Brindisi from La Traviata *– Oom-pah-pah, oom-pah-pah – and the three men sing. [Note: Please refer to page 3 for details on how to acquire the required performance track from Samuel French, Inc.])*

TITO.

LIBIAMO, LIBIAMO NE'LIETI CALICI
CHE LA BELLEZZA INFIORA.
E LA FUGGEVOL, FUGGEVOL ORA S'INEBRII
A VOLUTTÀ

CARLO.

LIBIAM NE'DOLCI FREMITI

MAX.

CHE SUSCITA L'AMORE,

TITO.

POICHÉ QUELL'OCHIO AL CORE ONNIPOTENTE VA.

ALL THREE.

LIBIAMO, AMORE, AMOR FRA I CALICI
PIÙ CALDI BACI AVRÀ. AH!

CHORUS. *(Which we hear as we do the orchestra.)*

LIBIAM, AMOR, FRA' CALICI
PIÙ CALDI BACI AVRÀ

CARLO.

TRA VOI TRA VOI SAPRÒ DIVIDERE
IL TEMPO MIO GIOCONDO;
TUTTO È FOLLIA, FOLLIA NEL MONDO
CIÒ CHE NON È PIACER

TITO.

GODIAM, FUGACE E RAPIDO

MAX.

E'IL GAUDIO DELL'AMORE,

CARLO & TITO.

E'UN FIOR CHE NASCE E MUORE,
NE PIÙ SI PUÒ GODER

ALL THREE.

GODIAMO, C'INVITA, C'INVITA UN FERVIDO
ACCENTO LUSINGHIER.

CHORUS.

GODIAMO, LA TAZZA, LA TAZZA E IL CANTICO,
LA NOTTE ABBELLA E IL RISO;
IN QUESTO, IN QUESTO PARADISO NE SCOPRA IL NUOVO DÌ

TITO.

LA VITA È NEL TRIPUDIO

MAX.

QUANDO NON S'AMI ANCORA

CARLO.

NOL DITE A CHI L'IGNORA,

ALL THREE.

E'IL MIO DESTIN COSÌ...

ALL THREE WITH CHORUS.

GODIAMO, LA TAZZA, LA TAZZA E IL CANTICO,
LA NOTTE ABBELLA E IL RISO;
IN QUESTO, IN QUESTO PARADISO
NE SCOPRA IL NUOVO DÌ
NE SCOPRA IL NUOVO DÌ
NE SCOPRA IL NUOVO DÌ!!

> *(When the number is over, they all laugh and celebrate: "Hoo!" "Haha!")*

CARLO. Whoa! That's so great! It makes you sweat. I'm a big sweater...

> *(**CARLO** pulls out the scarf he took from **MARIA** and wipes the sweat from his face and neck. **TITO** gapes in shock.)*

The trouble is, I sweat all over.

> *(He rubs the scarf on his crotch.)*

TITO. *AH! You! So it <u>was</u> you! For corrupting an innocent woman you will die!*

> (**TITO** *grabs the cheese knife and goes after* **CARLO**. *The Allegro from the overture to Verdi's opera* La Forza del Destino *plays as* **TITO** *chases* **CARLO** *around the room and out the door.*)

MAX. *Tito! No!*

CARLO. *He's crazy!*

SAUNDERS. *Stop it! What are you doing!*

TITO. *I kill you!*

MAX. *Tito, please! You're not in Italy anymore!*

> (*They're gone.*)

SAUNDERS. *(into the phone) Jacques! See if you can get Jussi back! …Well then page him at the airport! Tell him he can have MY mother if he really wants one! That'll teach him a lesson!*

> (*As he hangs up,* **MAX** *runs back in, through the front door, panting.*)

MAX. *Mr. Saunders! Help! I'm losing them!*

SAUNDERS. *Goddamit!*

> (*They run out through the front door –.*)

> (*At which moment,* **CARLO**, *panting, runs onto the patio, stage right. He looks around wildly. He starts to step into the room when he hears* **TITO** *and* **MARIA** *coming down the hall –.*)

MARIA. Tito! Stop. Tito!

> (*And* **CARLO** *runs away, back where he came from, as* **TITO** *and* **MARIA** *burst into the room.*)

TITO. I'm gonna kill him!

MARIA. Tito, what is happening?! Why are you angry?!

TITO. Because I saw you with that boy!

MARIA. Carlo?

TITO. Yeah, Carlo. And don't play goody-two-shoe with me. I lose a-my cookie.

MARIA. How did you find out about—

TITO. I saw you together, right here! You think you can hide these things from me?!

MARIA. Oh, Tito. Loosen up a little. He is nice a-young boy. And he's a hot a-pepper, eh? I'm a-crazy about him.

TITO. Oh, I can see *that.*

MARIA. And did you see that body of his? He is like a Greek God!

TITO. And that make you happy.

MARIA. It would make any woman happy. That boy is gonna give me some beautiful babies.

TITO. Agh!

MARIA. And this boyfriend is not exactly the first one, you know.

TITO. No?

MARIA. There have been three other at least. Maybe four, I have lost count.

TITO. *Ah.*

MARIA. But I think this one is worth keeping.

TITO. Keeping?

MARIA. You have to change with the time, Tito! Just think, we could live together as one a-big family!

TITO. "Family?" That's it. *That's it.* You want this boy in you life? Fine. Then I want a-divorce.

MARIA. What?

TITO. *Divorzio! Now! This a-minute!*

MARIA. Tito. You are overreacting.

TITO. *(in agony)* I love a-you so much, Maria.

MARIA. But we are still in love, Tito. There is just one more of us.

TITO. No! *I want a-divorce, divorce!*

MARIA. *You are a-crazy!*

TITO. *I WANT A-DIVORCE!*

MARIA. *(steaming mad)* Okay, that's a-fine! That's a-peachy! *All these years, I take a-care of you! I cook! I clean! I wait at* *rehearsal, I wait at performance! You snore at night, you smell in the morning! You drive a-me crazy and I put up with you!*

TITO. *So we get a-divorce!*

MARIA. *NO! WE GET A-TWO DIVORCE! I WANT A-ONE, TOO!*

(**SAUNDERS** *and* **MAX** *run in.*)

SAUNDERS. Mrs. Merelli! Have you seen – *Tito.* Oh, thank God! Now listen to me. I realize there was a misunderstanding –

TITO. Is not a problem, because I *quit!*

SAUNDERS. Excuse me?

TITO. I said I *quit,* I am *finished, I stay here no more!*

SAUNDERS. But you can't quit! The performance starts in less than two hours!

MAX. Maria, stop him!

MARIA. *No! Let him go! Let him have his stage a-door, with his girls and his picture!*

TITO. *I quit, I quit!*

CARLO. *(appearing at the door)* No, *I* quit!

TITO. You!

CARLO. Yeah me. And you're crazy because what I did was perfectly normal!

TITO. Normal?! You ruin the family *and that's a-normal?*

SAUNDERS. Gentlemen, I'm sure we can solve this little –

TITO, CARLO, MARIA. *SHUT UP!*

TITO. Maria, good-bye!

(*He goes out the front door, slamming it behind him.*)

MARIA. That's it. I have had enough. *I am finished with him!* I will go to Assisi and become a nun. But first I will go to Chanel and spend his money.

(*She exits out the front door and slams it behind her.*)

SAUNDERS. Carlo, please listen to me –

CARLO. No!

SAUNDERS. Please!

CARLO. Forget it!

SAUNDERS. I need you!

CARLO. Never!

SAUNDERS. I'll double your fee.

CARLO. No.

SAUNDERS. Triple your fee.

CARLO. I have integrity! I'm an artist! I can't be bought!

SAUNDERS. Ten times your fee!

CARLO. *(tilts his head and thinks hard)* ...No. I will not be involved with a man who tried to strangle me. Goodbye!

> *(He exits, slamming the front door.)*

MAX. *Wait!*

SAUNDERS. *Wait!*

MAX. *Wait!*

SAUNDERS. *You can't do this!*

MAX. *Stop!*

SAUNDERS & MAX. *STOP!*

> *(But he's gone.)*

MAX. They're gone.

SAUNDERS. *Jesus Christ, now what do we do?*

MAX. *I-I-I don't know, sir. It's only two hours till the curtain.*

SAUNDERS. *Jesus Christ.*

MAX. Of course you've still got me. Don't forget *that.*

> *(SAUNDERS looks at MAX and starts crying.)*

SAUNDERS. Sorry, Max. You're a good man. You're honest. You're loyal. You're going to be the father of my grandchild.

> *(He cries again.)*

You don't know how hard I've fought for this, Max. I was born in Akron, Ohio. Can you imagine what that was like? T.S. Eliot wrote *The Wasteland* thinking about

Akron, Ohio. The town had one piano and they used it as a planter. But even then I said no. No! This will not be the only life ahead of me. This will not define who I am. I want music. I want culture. I want to bring opera to the people. And now when I have the one chance to do exactly what I've dreamed about, where the hell is my tenor, Max! *I need a tenor!*

> *(At this moment, we hear a huge, lusty tenor voice outside the front door, coming down the hall, singing "O Sole Mio." It sounds like Pavarotti in his prime. The enormous voice is full of joy and sunlight. As* **SAUNDERS** *and* **MAX** *hear it, they're first confused, then amazed, then in shock, and finally joyous over finding their solution:)*

VOICE. *(singing, offstage)*
MA N'ATU SOLE
CCHIÙ BELLO, OJE NE'.

> *(speaking, offstage)*

Scusi, signora, coming through.

> *(singing, offstage)*

O SOLE
O SOLE MIO
STA 'FRONTE A TE!
STA 'NFRONTE A TE!

> *(He knocks on the door; speaking, offstage:)*

Hello?! I have a-you luggage.

> *(When the man who is singing gets no answer, he opens the door and backs in, pulling a luggage cart filled with the Merellis' luggage. The luggage cart stays outside the door at this point.)*

> *(He turns around and we see a tough, likeable, Italian man of simple origins – a former Gondolier, a street-worker, wearing the uniform and cap of a bellhop.)*

(The man's name is **BEPPO** *and he is a bellhop at the hotel. He has a heavy Italian accent full of the rich guttural sounds of a lifetime of drinking and good living.)*

(He turns and sees **SAUNDERS** *and* **MAX** *gaping at him.)*

(And what they see is an absolute dead-ringer for **TITO**. *It's like the very same man, except that* **BEPPO** *has a moustache. He is played by the same actor who plays* **TITO**.)*

BEPPO. Forgive a-da singing, is just a-da bellhop.

MAX. The bellhop?

BEPPO. I know. What a world! *Ha Haaaa!*

*(***MAX** *and* **SAUNDERS** *look at each other and get the same idea at the same moment. We hear the sound of a small bright bell. Ping!)*

(The swelling sounds of "O sole mio" fill the air as the stage goes black.)

End of Act One

ACT TWO

(Ten minutes later. In the darkness we hear **BEPPO***'s huge tenor voice singing the last thirty seconds of the aria "Recondita Armonia" from Puccini's* Tosca. *The sound is magnificent and it fills the theatre.)*

(An instant after the last note, while it is still reverberating, the lights pop on and we see **BEPPO** *with his arms outstretched in the gesture of a born performer.* **SAUNDERS** *and* **MAX** *are looking at him, their mouths open in astonishment.)*

(By this time, the luggage cart is on stage, having been pulled on by **BEPPO** *during the ten minutes between the acts.)*

BEPPO. Good enough?

SAUNDERS. Yes. Yes, I'd say that's good enough.

MAX. And you're the bellhop?

BEPPO. That's right.

> *(During the following,* **BEPPO** *starts to take the luggage off the luggage cart.)*

SAUNDERS. And you understand what happened.

BEPPO. Yah. Signor Merelli, he leave-a-da-concert, and I'm a-gonna sing for him.

MAX. Exactly.

BEPPO. Ha haaaa! That's a-good! I like to sing in front of people. It make them happy. It give a-them pleasure.

SAUNDERS. Good –

BEPPO. I was gondoliere in Venezia, eh? Every day I pole a-da boat through the mud of my country and I sing

43

BEPPO. *(singing)*

  O SOLE MIO –

SAUNDERS. Excellent. Now I said that we lost a singer, but in fact we lost *two* singers, so you and Max will carry the entire weight of the concert. You'll be our soloists.

BEPPO. I like that. "Soloist."

SAUNDERS. So the idea is that you will each start out with a few solo numbers, then you'll join together in the second half and sing some duets – if you know them, of course.

BEPPO. Like what?

MAX. Uh, "O Mimì," "Sì pel ciel," the *Don Carlo* –

BEPPO. Ha ha! Of course I know. Are you joking? That's a-my life. My blood. You want to see?

    (He pulls out a knife.)

I show you the blood in my veins, it has a-music inside! You see the notes a-go by that have come a-from my heart!

MAX. We got it –

SAUNDERS. *(taken aback at the knife) Thank* you – Mr. uh…?

BEPPO. Beppo. Just Beppo. My father name is a-Beppo, too. And his father. And my uncle. All in *Venezia,* the greatest city in the world, the town of my people, my soul, my family, my life's own –

SAUNDERS. *I understand!* Now listen to me. The concert starts in less than an hour, and we're on a *tight schedule.*

BEPPO. Tight is good. I like to *do* things *fast.* Bim-Bam. Like American movie.

SAUNDERS. Good –

BEPPO. I like a-Robin Hood with a-Douglas Fairbank. *Wsht! Wsht!*

MAX. I like that one, too!

BEPPO. He is man of honor, like me. He inspire people who need his help because honor is the most important thing a man can possess. If you have a-no honor, you have *nothing*.

SAUNDERS. *Thank* you. So here's the plan: you take a shower, freshen up and shave off that moustache –

BEPPO. *(at the food buffet)* Is this food a-for me?

MAX. Help yourself.

SAUNDERS. But are you *listening?!*

BEPPO. *(mouth full)* I hear everything.

SAUNDERS. So you'll freshen up, with Max to help you –

MAX. I'll be here the whole time, don't worry.

BEPPO. But Mr. Merelli, he may not like that I take his place, eh?

SAUNDERS. Don't worry, he owes me one, believe me.

BEPPO. Because he leave the concert.

MAX & SAUNDERS. Right.

BEPPO. "Tito Merelli." Ha! I see his name on poster. And I hear of him. He is big singer. He is good, uh, how you say, *a-simbolo* for the people of my country –

SAUNDERS. Good –

BEPPO. Italia, the land of my father, the land of honor, the land of –

SAUNDERS. *Would you get moving!* We have a *time* problem!

BEPPO. I *hate* time problem, they are bad! A man should relax and have a good life. Live a-well, eat a-well, and enjoy his wife. I had a good wife, she pass away. I love her so deep. In bed she was like machine, her pistons pumping like –

SAUNDERS. *WOULD YOU JUST STOP TALKING!*

BEPPO. He is always like this?

MAX. He's my father-in-law.

BEPPO. I pity you.

MAX. Thanks.

SAUNDERS. *Would you please just go!*

BEPPO. Okay, okay! I'm a-move! Wait! Do I get paid for this?

SAUNDERS. Of course you get paid. I'll pay you exactly what I was paying Tito since he's not getting it. Five thousand dollars.

BEPPO. Whoa! Is a lot of money. Is injustice.

SAUNDERS. You're telling me.

BEPPO. I have to carry luggage for years to make all this money. Okay, I make decision. I am changing job. From now on I am not Beppo the Bellhop, I am Beppo the Singer. This concert launch my career. It is beginning of whole new life for me, where my family is proud, my city *Venezia*, my people, my country –

SAUNDERS. *(pushing* **BEPPO** *into the bedroom) Get in the shower, or you'll be Beppo the Unemployed!*

(**SAUNDERS** *slams the door.*)

BEPPO. *(from offstage)* Okay! Shower! Shave! Suit! *Avanti!*

MAX. Sir, it's uncanny. He's a dead ringer!

SAUNDERS. He's a pain in the neck! But oh my God, we're saved! And nobody will even know the difference!

MAX. But couldn't you get arrested for fraud or something?

SAUNDERS. Of course not! That's why it's perfect! We're not going to *say* he's Tito. The announcer will say "And now please welcome the star of the evening!" clap, clap, clap, he comes out on stage and they'll *think* he's Tito! But listen to me: No one must ever know a thing about this. Is that clear?!

MAX. But what if Tito's upset about it?

SAUNDERS. Upset? He's breaking his contract! I could sue him for a million dollars! Now you stay here with Beppo and clean him up fast. I'll go see Jacques and fill him in.

(*He hurries to the door, turns, and chuckles happily.*)

From this point on, Max, nothing can go wrong!

(**SAUNDERS** *exits, slamming the door behind him. Ring!* **MAX** *picks up the phone.*)

MAX. Hi, I'm sorry, but we're busy at the m – …Maggie? Oh Maggie, sweetheart, how *are* you?! How are you *feeling*?! Oh, I've felt so terrible being away this week and –…

What? Contractions? You're having contractions? Oh my God, are you sure?!

Maggie, where are you?! Are you in the hospital?! But the doctor said it would be ten more days before the baby came, he *told* me that! You *heard* him say it! Can't you just cross your legs or something?!

Oh, Maggie, God, I wish I were there – …Maggie?

(He clicks the phone like mad; he's lost the line.)

Maggie, can you hear me? …MAGGIE!

*(**BEPPO** hurries in from the bedroom soaking wet, wearing a towel.)*

BEPPO. *Max! Come quick! The stopper don't work and the bathroom is a-flood!*

MAX. I-I-I-I-I can't right now. *She's having contractions!*

BEPPO. What's a contractions?

MAX. My wife.

BEPPO. Your wife?

MAX. Maggie. She's pregnant. And she's almost there! Just do your best. I've got to call her. And tell Mr. Saunders. *I'll be back in a minute!*

*(**MAX** runs out. **BEPPO** squares his shoulders and marches back to the bedroom. The moment he's gone, **MIMI** enters through the front door holding a script. She wears the costume of a street urchin from the 18th Century. She rushes down front and poses dramatically.)*

MIMI. *(with great drama and tears)* "Your Majesty, please! You are the Queen and I but a peasant, but oh, dear God, my family is starving! 'LET THEM EAT CAKE?!!' WE CAN HARDLY AFFORD A BOWL OF GRUEL!"

CARLO. *(offstage)* Mimi!?

(He enters.)

CARLO. Mimi, where have you – Holy cow, what's that?

MIMI. It's a costume. Do you want to ask me why I'm wearing it? Because I got the part, I got the part, *I got the part!!*

> **(MIMI** *screams with happiness and hugs him and twirls him around.)*

Oh, Carlo! I'm an actress now, *a working actress!* You see MGM is filming a movie here in Paris called *Marie Antoinette* and I play a peasant girl, I mean I'm not the star, but I have one good scene with Norma Shearer!, and they want me to wear this costume to get used to it because we start filming tomorrow and the actress who was going to play the part got sick and they auditioned over twenty girls *and they picked me!*

CARLO. They must be very smart.

MIMI. *(modestly)* Oh I don't know…

> *(She gets tears in her eyes.)*

It's just that I worked so hard for this and I gave up so much! I mean that's what we do, we're in the theatre – and I actually signed the contract, and the doctor did a physical for insurance and they gave me the script

> *(She's weeping now.)*

and I talked to the director and he said he was glad to have me! I am so happy.

> *(They embrace.)*

I didn't think it would happen. I have a profession!

> *(Still crying, she wipes her eyes.)*

Oh, I'm so stupid. My mascara's running. Have you met my father yet?

CARLO. I have.

MIMI. And does he like you?

CARLO. I wouldn't say so, no.

MIMI. Oh he will. I promise he will!

> *(She throws her arms around* **CARLO** *– at which moment,* **BEPPO** *enters from the bedroom, shaved, his hair combed, his moustache gone, and he's wearing one of* **TITO** *'s dressing gowns. So now he looks 100 percent like* **TITO**. *Except, perhaps, for the glint in his eye.)*

> *(***BEPPO** *and the lovers gasp in surprise. There is an instant when* **MIMI** *hesitates about her father.)*

MIMI. Daddy?

> *(***BEPPO** *looks around for this "Daddy" – then gets it.)*

BEPPO. Yah?

MIMI. *(bravely)* Oh, Daddy, please listen and keep an open mind. I know how protective you are and how you don't think I'm ready to get involved with a man yet, but I am, I really am, I promise, and this is him, he's the man I love! Daddy, Carlo.

> *(Beat. Then* **BEPPO** *walks up and shakes* **CARLO** *'s hand.)*

BEPPO. How are you, my boy?

CARLO. I'm… I'm fine, sir. You?

BEPPO. I am feeling tip a-top, thank you.

CARLO. We really are in love with each other, sir, and I'm very sorry we got off on the wrong foot. I'm not sure what I did to offend you, but if there's anything I can do to make it up to you –

BEPPO. No. You are good boy. I respect you.

CARLO. Really?

MIMI. Oh I just knew he'd like you! I knew it!

BEPPO. You two make a-beautiful couple, eh? And you will make a-beautiful children together.

MIMI. Oh, Daddy!

BEPPO. You are in love with each other. That is all that matters.

> *(Perhaps in the background we hear "O mio babbino caro" from Puccini's* Gianni Schicchi.*)*

I see how you touch each other, how you hold her hand, how you glance at him out of the corner of your eye, right here. And look how you smile at each other – I caught you, eh? – because words need not be spoken between you. I was in love like this just once in my life and I am happy for you.

MIMI. Oh, I love you!

> *(She hugs* **BEPPO**.*)*

Oh, Daddy, I've never seen you like this. It's a whole new side of you and I love it so much!

> *(She hugs him again. When she's finished, he hugs her – putting his hand on her backside. He enjoys holding this beautiful woman.)*

CARLO. Sir, can I ask you something: you were so angry before. What made you change your mind?

BEPPO. Boh. Who knows. Perhaps I was a-feel a-pressure, eh? When we grow up, we feel sometime too much is happening. You see what I mean? But when fortune smile on us, we are more *profondo,* how you say, deep. Rich. We hear the music that God gave to us to heal ourselves, eh? If I was unkind to you, then please forgive me.

CARLO. You're amazing. You're just –

> *(***MAX** *hurries in.)*

MAX. Carlo!

CARLO. Hey Max, listen. I know it's late, but do you think I could get back in the concert tonight?

MAX. Are you kidding? Of course you can!

CARLO. I have my tux downstairs.

MAX. Then go, quick, put it on. I'll tell my father-in-law, he'll be thrilled.

CARLO. You got it!

MIMI. I'll come with you!

CARLO. *(calling back) I'll see you in a minute!*

> (**MIMI** *and* **CARLO** *run out together.* **MAX** *looks at* **BEPPO** *and for an instant he isn't sure if it's* **TITO** *or* **BEPPO**.*)*

MAX. Beppo?

BEPPO. Max.

MAX. You look great.

BEPPO. How is your wife, Moggie?

MAX. She's all right. Thanks. I-I talked to the doctor and he thinks it was a false alarm, and since I go home tomorrow, I should be back there when –

BEPPO. When the head come *bang* right out of the –

MAX. Right! That's it.

BEPPO. It is called the canal. I know all about canal, I am from Venice.

MAX. Well at least I'll be there.

BEPPO. Good. Is important. You are husband first and then the singer.

MAX. I know. It's hard sometimes.

BEPPO. You are telling me.

MAX. But listen, I've got to go tell Mr. Saunders about Carlo, so can I trust you to put your tuxedo on, please?

BEPPO. Puh! Of course. I change a-like lightning. *Wsht! Wsht!* I move like a-Robin Hood in the forest, *pom-pom!*, and nothing can a-stop me, because, like him, I have the will to succeed, to be a hero for my people!

MAX. We're going to be friends, aren't we.

BEPPO. The best.

MAX. Great. I'll be back in a minute.

> (**MAX** *runs out.*)

BEPPO. *(calling to* **MAX***) I am from the forest! Wsht! Wsht! I save a-the day!*

(He turns to the food.)

BEPPO. But first I eat a good meal, eh? It make sense. I need a-strength to sing, I need a-muscle.

(He goes to the buffet.)

Mm. This look a-nice. Is hard to find a good tongue these days.

(He holds the tongue up so they can have a conversation.)

How do you, Mr. Tongue, is nice to meet you.

(as the tongue, in a high squeaky voice:)

"Is nice to meet you."

(as **BEPPO***:)*

Where is the rest of you?

(as the tongue:)

"I sacrifice my body so you can have a good lunch."

(as **BEPPO***:)*

Thank you, Tongue, you are very noble. Sometime we have to give up something we love in order to make someone else happy. That is why I gave up singing, eh? It was a-my dream, but then I had to make some money for my family, eh?

(as the tongue:)

"You are philosopher. You should be successful man by this time."

(as **BEPPO***:)*

You are telling me. Maybe this concert is my big a-chance.

(as the tongue:)

"I think it is, so you should not fuck it up like you usually do."

(as **BEPPO***:)*

Thank you for being such an honest tongue.

*(He kisses the tongue, then takes a bite out of it – at which point, **MARIA** strides in through the front door. She is wearing sunglasses.)*

MARIA. Tito.

BEPPO. *(his mouth full)* Nmmf?

MARIA. Tito, be quiet. I need to say something.

BEPPO. Nommf kumpht –

MARIA. *Just listen!* I have something important to say and is difficult. Do not interrupt me.

BEPPO. That will be hard for me.

MARIA. I know, but you must hear everything I have to say. I have made a decision. Tito, where are all those happy times we used to spend together, eh? Where does such love go so fast, you tell me. Does it fly away? It seem impossible. For how many years do we stand up for each other and a-cheer for each other. Okay, so we yell and we scream and the vein a-pop out of you neck like a fire hose, but is that so bad? It is *life*, Tito! We are pulsing with life! And I make a confession, now, okay? I want it back. I want all of it back, so here's a-my plan: We go into that bedroom and make a-crazy, passionate love like we used to. We possess each other, we become each other. Hands, lips, bodies, we hold nothing back – and *then* you ask a-youself, "Is this marriage worth a-saving?" What do you think?

BEPPO. To me, this is a very good plan.

*(**BEPPO** kisses her with tremendous sexual energy. When it's over, she can hardly stand up.)*

MARIA. Give me ten a-minute.

BEPPO. Okay.

(She exits into to the bedroom stage left and closes the door.)

*(Instantly, **RACÓN** enters through the front door. She is ravishingly beautiful, dressed superbly in*

silks and jewelry that fit her like a second skin. She speaks with a heavy Russian accent.)

RACÓN. Tito. It is I, Racón.

(She kisses him on the mouth.)

Do you remember?

BEPPO. It is coming back to me.

RACÓN. I am performink here in Paris this week, and am hearing that you are in city for concert. So I am askink myself, is it time to come see Tito after all these years. What do you think?

BEPPO. You made good decision.

RACÓN. I am likink your hotel. Is beink beautiful. Do you spend much time here?

BEPPO. Is like second home.

RACÓN. You look the same, Tito. You have not changed.

BEPPO. You would be surprised.

RACÓN. It is many years since we are seeink each other.

BEPPO. Yet you are even more beautiful than the day we met.

RACÓN. I am flattered.

BEPPO. I am honored.

RACÓN. I am impressed.

BEPPO. I am overwhelmed. Are you hungry?

RACÓN. I am ravenous.

BEPPO. Good because my producer have put out big spread for me. You like a-spread?

RACÓN. I am liking spread.

BEPPO. Would you like a-some tongue?

RACÓN. I am loving tongue.

BEPPO. *(Holding up the tongue and using Mr. Tongue's squeaky voice.)* "I am glad you love me. Sometime I get very lonely on the plate by myself."

RACÓN. I am understanding, my little tongue. I am lonely too. But in Russia, everyone is lonely.

BEPPO. *(as Mr. Tongue.)* "You should have been born in Venezia like me. You would be happier person."

RACÓN. You are telling me.

(They laugh. He touches her cheek. She presses her cheek to his hand.)

BEPPO. Wait. I put on recording for atmosphere. Don't go 'way.

(He goes to the record player.)

This remind me of moment in *La Bohème* when Rodolfo meet Mimì in Paris, eh? Their fingers touch, their hearts become one, so they sing together softly at the top of their lung.

(The recording starts playing. It is the ravishing duet "O Soave Fanciulla" from La Bohème. *They take it in. This is their life's blood.)*

RACÓN. Puccini.

BEPPO. Puccini.

RACÓN. My recordink with Slezak. You are thinking of me. *Ya znayu.*

(She wanders to the balcony.)

Is beautiful night. The people arrive down below for concert. You must be proud.

BEPPO. Poh. For me is old hat. Still, I would like to do well at this one.

(She takes his hand.)

Remind me: you are married now?

RACÓN. No. It is my dream. Men are beink afraid of me, I am not knowing why.

BEPPO. Because you are strong woman. You are beautiful like goddess. They are afraid you will devour them. But to me you are gentle. You are *delicata.* Like a flower.

RACÓN. Perhaps I could be joining you at end of concert for duet.

BEPPO. I would like that very much. And my producer will pay you big money. He like to pay out lots of money, it make him happy.

(They share a laugh.)

You are the most beautiful creature I ever see.

RACÓN. Oh, Tito. You are remembering the happy times we had here in Paris together?

BEPPO. I remember like a-yesterday.

RACÓN. The lights of the city.

BEPPO. The water.

RACÓN. The walks.

BEPPO. The food.

RACÓN. Our son.

BEPPO. Our son. Our son?

RACÓN. The little boy we saw playing on bank of river and we are saying "oh, if we are having child some day he will be just like this one."

BEPPO. Of course. And I would like such a boy. I would play soccer with him and show him American movie.

RACÓN. But would you take so much time from big career to be having son like this?

BEPPO. Is what I dream of at night when my eyes are closing.

RACÓN. Oh Tito, me too! I am wanting child so badly now!

(She throws herself at him and kisses him deeply.)

You have changed so much. You are whole new man!

MARIA. *(offstage)* Tito!! Are you ready?

BEPPO. *(calling)* Uno momento.

RACÓN. Who is that?

BEPPO. My mother. She travel with me to do the cleaning.

RACÓN. What about your wife?

BEPPO. She is dead.

RACÓN. Dead? Since when?

BEPPO. Not so long ago.

RACÓN. *Oh, Tito!*

>   *(She leaps on top of him and smothers him with kisses.)*

I am thinking where is bedroom.

BEPPO. That is quite a coincidence.

RACÓN. Be giving me five minutes.

BEPPO. Okay.

>   *(She disappears into the bedroom stage right and closes the door.* BEPPO *is alone onstage.)*

I have spent many years in the wilderness, but I think the drought is a-finally over. I begin as gondolier in Venezia when I am eight years old, one of fourteen children, and I felt a-very lucky. I pole the boat through the dark canal and I sing about life – and what do you know?, the more I sing, the better I become. So I move to Paris to be in the opera, but life is life and I become bellhop. It is not what I hope for, but it is also not, how you say?, *infelice.* It is not unhappy. I do honest work and get honest pay. But suddenly life has done somersault. In that room is Russian tiger waiting to pounce all over me; and over there is Italian antelope wanting to devour my body without a-mercy. Meanwhile, I am living in hotel suite with marble bathroom, and I just eat my first good meal in a-three weeks. Life is a-full of surprises, eh? The trick is to be patient. You take a deep breath, you thank God for all the things you have, you wait a-you turn, and then, like a miracle, life come to you.

>   *(MARIA opens her bedroom door.)*

MARIA. Tito. I am ready for you.

>   *(She exits, and* RACÓN *opens her door.)*

RACÓN. In Russia we are beink very efficient. I am ready when you are.

>   *(She exits, closing the door.)*

BEPPO. And now I must make decision, eh? The wife or the lover. Of course it is someone else's wife, but to Italian man that is technicality.

(*At which moment,* **SAUNDERS** *enters through the front door.*)

SAUNDERS. Beppo, how's it going? Have you found –? *Beppo! You haven't changed?!*

BEPPO. I have not had time!

SAUNDERS. *Are you insane?!*

BEPPO. I am not so sure.

SAUNDERS. *We have less than thirty minutes!*

BEPPO. The time pulled away from me like Italian racehorse flying toward finish line. He intend to cross it, but then he see a beautiful mare in the meadow, flicking her tail in invitation so he say to himself, "Racehorse, you deserve some pleasure, and this is not the hay you eat for lunch every day –"

SAUNDERS. *What are you talking about?! Just get the hell in there and change! Now!*

(**SAUNDERS** *points to the bedroom with* **MARIA**.)

BEPPO. My clothes are in there.

(*He points to the bedroom with* **RACÓN**.)

SAUNDERS. Then get in there and take your clothes off!

BEPPO. Is my intention.

(**BEPPO** *disappears into the bedroom where* **RACÓN** *is waiting.*)

(*At which moment,* **MAX** *runs in.*)

MAX. Mr. Saunders! Sir! There's trouble with the programs!

SAUNDERS. The programs?

MAX. They printed them upside-down. They look like they're in Chinese or something.

SAUNDERS. Goddamit!

(*He bangs on the door of* **BEPPO**'s *bedroom.*)

Hey! How's it going in there?

BEPPO. *(offstage) Pretty good.*

SAUNDERS. Come soon.

BEPPO. *(offstage) I am doing my best!*

> *(SAUNDERS and MAX run out the door, passing MIMI on the way.)*

MIMI. Hi, Max, Mr. Saunders –

MAX. Sorry, we gotta go!

> *(And they're gone – at which moment.)*

> *(Ring!)*

> *(The telephone rings and MIMI answers it.)*

MIMI. Hello? Yes, it is Mimi. Oh *hello, MGM!* Yes I'm very excited about the movie.

> *(She's beaming.)*

Sure, I'd love some news. Am I sitting down? Oh I'm sure I don't have to sit down to hear anything you have to –

> *(She listens, and then she gasps and her legs give way.)*

What? Are you *sure?* Yes I did do all the medical tests and the examination, and… I'm having a baby?

> *(She touches her stomach.)*

Oh stop it, is this a joke? Who is this really? It is? Are you positive? Yes, I will see my doctor.

> *(The phone falls from her hand but she manages to get it back in the cradle. She looks bewildered. At this moment, TITO hurries in through the front door.)*

TITO. Mimi, there you are!

MIMI. Daddy? Oh, Daddy, there's something I have to tell you!

TITO. No, let me go first! Mimi, I know this will be hard for you, but – *I don't know how to tell you this!*

MIMI. What? What happened?

TITO. Your mother and I

> *(sob)*

are getting a divorce.

MIMI. A divorce? I don't believe it.

TITO. Is true.

MIMI. But what happened? Daddy! I know you two fight a lot, but –

TITO. No. Is something else, I… *I cannot tell you!*

MIMI. You have to tell me.

TITO. No.

MIMI. Yes!

TITO. *No!*

MIMI. *Please!*

TITO. Okay. I have just discovered that your mother is having an affair.

MIMI. Mother? Oh stop it.

TITO. Is true.

MIMI. That's impossible!

TITO. She told me herself! She *discussed* it with me to my face! And what is worse, *I caught them together.*

MIMI. Oh, Daddy. This is awful. I'm so sorry! Who is it?

TITO. Is Carlo Nucci.

MIMI. *(a scream, crumpling to the floor) AHHHH!* Is this a joke?

TITO. No.

MIMI. Carlo?

TITO. Yah.

MIMI. The *singer* Carlo?

TITO. Yah. Do you know him?

MIMI. *I'M IN LOVE WITH HIM!*

TITO. *No! Since when?*

MIMI. For over a year! It's been a year!

TITO. You love Carlo Nucci?

MIMI. I did –

TITO. *(hugging her)* Oh my little girl, I'm a-*so sorry.*

MIMI. But you *liked* him! You said you *liked* him! And you were so sweet and loving!

TITO. I tried to be nice to him, but then I *caught* them together! I *saw* them! And your mother *admit* it to me!

MIMI. Oh my God! Oh my God!

   (She reels towards the door.)

TITO. Where are you going?

MIMI. To the doctor!

TITO. *Mimi, I'm a-sorry!!*

   (**MIMI** *runs out the door just as* **SAUNDERS** *hurries in.)*

SAUNDERS. I cannot believe the incompetence of –

   (He sees **TITO** *and gasps.)*

 Oh my God. Beppo. I just told you to change.

   (The following goes very rapidly.)

TITO. What?

SAUNDERS. Where's the tuxedo?!

TITO. What tuxedo?

SAUNDERS. *Your* tuxedo!

TITO. I dunno.

SAUNDERS. You're supposed to be wearing it!

TITO. I am?

SAUNDERS. Yes!

TITO. The tux?

SAUNDERS. Yes!

TITO. What tux?

SAUNDERS. Your tux!

TITO. Why?

SAUNDERS. For the concert!

TITO. What concert?

SAUNDERS. *Our concert!*

> *(steaming mad)*

Listen to me. Do you want to make something of yourself or not? It's your choice. You can either sing at the concert and make five thousand dollars or you can drag out your life singing "O Solo Mio" in hotel hallways, which is exactly where you're headed at the moment! *You're an opportunist! And you talk too much!* Now straighten up! Put your shoulders back and act like a man!

TITO. Have you lost a-you mind?

SAUNDERS. All right. That's it. We have fifteen minutes, *now march into that bedroom and take your clothes off!*

> *(**TITO** walks into the bedroom where **MARIA** is waiting and closes the door.)*

> *(At which moment, **MAX** runs in.)*

MAX. *Sir! Please! Come quick!*

SAUNDERS. What now?

MAX. It's the conductor!

SAUNDERS. The young guy?

MAX. Yes! He's walking out!

SAUNDERS. Why?

MAX. He says he won't be part of a second-rate effort because it won't serve the music.

SAUNDERS. Serve the –? You tell that little nobody that I'll sue his skinny little American backside from here to kingdom come! What's his name again?

MAX. Leonard Bernstein.

SAUNDERS. Well he'll never work again. Come on!

> *(They run out.)*

> *(At which moment, **RACÓN** and **BEPPO** come reeling out of their bedroom, both disheveled, their clothes in disarray, their hair tousled.)*

RACÓN. Tito! You are amazing man! I am remembering from before the passion and strength but have no recollection of animal noises.

BEPPO. That was you.

(RACÓN holds her hand to her mouth in surprise, then laughs. BEPPO heads for the other bedroom.)

RACÓN. Where are you going?

BEPPO. I must dress a-for concert or have very angry man yell at me.

RACÓN. Not yet! Come back! Please!

(She pushes him back into their bedroom. She remains in the living room and talks to him through the open doorway. If possible, we see BEPPO's hand in the doorway, holding the door jamb.)

BEPPO. *(offstage)* But I must change clothing!

RACÓN. No! Time is standing still for us. We are in fairy kingdom now.

BEPPO. *(offstage)* Tell that to Mr. Sander.

RACÓN. You are Eugene Onegin and I am beautiful country girl and we are longing for each other as in Tchaikovsky opera. Then, when you are sick with desire, I will twist around you like Russian ivy twist around strong Russian elm tree. Then I will separate bark from trunk until tree is naked and submitting to fairy goddess of the Russian forest.

BEPPO. *(offstage)* Now that you mention it, I have some time.

(RACÓN enters the bedroom, closing the door behind her.)

(Instantly the door to the other bedroom opens and TITO and MARIA reel into the room, disheveled, their clothes in disarray, their hair tousled. MARIA is in a slip.)

*(Note: this is the moment when, hopefully, through the use of a stage manager's hand and a recording of **BEPPO**'s voice in the bedroom, we give the audience the happy shock of a magic trick – that the actor playing **BEPPO/TITO** was stage right at one moment, and then instantly stage left.)*

TITO. Maria, what has happened to you? You are new woman!

MARIA. That's what I'm a-telling you. You never listen to me.

TITO. But I am angry at you!

MARIA. Then *show* me, Tito. Show me your anger and displeasure. Show me now!

(She pushes him back into the bedroom, slamming the door behind them.)

*(At which moment, **CARLO** appears at the front door, wearing his tux. He's in a wonderful mood.)*

CARLO. Mimi? ...Mimi?

*(He opens the door to the bedroom down stage right and sees **RACÓN** and **BEPPO** on the bed.)*

Ahh!

(Slams the door, shocked.)

Sorry. Sorry. My fault. Sorry. Oh my God...

*(**MIMI** enters through the front door, angry and in distress.)*

Mimi! There you are. Listen, don't go into that bedroom.

MIMI. Why? Is my *mother* in there?!

CARLO. No. That's the problem. I wish she *were*.

(Whap! She slaps him across the face as hard as she can.)

Ow! What was that for?!

(Whap!)

Oww!

MIMI. I thought you were such a nice guy!

CARLO. I am a nice guy! What the hell is this about?!

> *(She tries to hit him again, but he holds her arm.)*

MIMI. I've heard about what's going on and I'm not putting up with it!

CARLO. Listen, I've got to warn you, I did some boxing when I was in –

> *(Whap!)*

Oww!!

MIMI. You're not really a man at all! You're a tenor!

CARLO. What is the matter with you! You're babbling!

MIMI. *How could you do this to me?!*

CARLO. *Do what to you?!*

MIMI. *She's my mother!*

CARLO. Forget your mother, it's your father I'm worried about.

MIMI. *AND YOU SHOULD BE, BECAUSE HE'LL KILL YOU FOR THIS!*

CARLO. *WHAT ARE YOU TALKING ABOUT?!*

> *(**BEPPO** enters from the bedroom.)*

BEPPO. Hey, what's a-with noise? A person cannot – …Mimi! How are you, my love? You two are happy?

RACÓN. *(at the door)* Tito. Come to bed.

BEPPO. You will have to excuse me. As you can see, I have a-the unfinished business.

> *(**BEPPO** exits into the bedroom, closing the door behind him. **MIMI** is dumbstruck.)*

MIMI. Daddy? …*Daddy, what are you doing in there?!* Oh my God! What's happening?!

> *(**MARIA** enters from the other bedroom. She is now dressed for the concert.)*

MARIA. Mimi?

MIMI. Mother!

MARIA. Carlo.

CARLO. Mrs. Merelli.

MIMI. "Mrs. Merelli?" That's not what you've been calling her lately, now is it?

CARLO. What are you talking about?!

MIMI. *I'm talking about the two of you!*

MARIA. The two of us what?

> (**RACÓN** *gives a shout of laughter from the guest bedroom.*)

MARIA. Who is that?

CARLO. Nobody.

MIMI. Nobody!

CARLO. You don't want to know.

MIMI. Mother, don't go in there.

> (**MARIA** *opens the door and sees* **RACÓN** *and* **BEPPO** *together on the bed. She screams, staggers backwards and faints onto the sofa.*)

MIMI. *Mother!*

CARLO. *Mrs. Merelli!*

MIMI. *Mother, say something!*

> (**RACÓN** *comes running out of the bedroom to help.*)

RACÓN. Ay! Oh the poor woman. Be giving her room, she is fainting.

> (**MAX** *and* **SAUNDERS** *appear at the door, see* **MARIA** *on the sofa and rush over.*)

MAX. Maria?

SAUNDERS. Oh my God.

MAX. Is she all right?!

SAUNDERS. What happened?

RACÓN. It is Tito's mother. She fainted.

> (*At this,* **MARIA** *opens her eyes and rears up.*)

MARIA. *Mother?! Who say I'm his mother?!*

RACÓN. Tito.

> (**MARIA** *faints again – at which moment* **TITO**
> *enters from the master bedroom and sees* **MARIA** *on
> the floor.*)

TITO. Maria? *Maria, what happen?! Oh, Maria, say something!
Who did this to you! I will kill him!*

MARIA. Tito?

RACÓN. Tito?

CARLO. How did you do that?

MIMI. Is this a trick?

TITO. Tatiana! What are you doing here?

RACÓN. I am hearing you are in Paris for concert and am
thinking of joining you on stage tonight.

SAUNDERS. You'd do that, really?

RACÓN. If he is wanting me.

TITO. Of course I want you.

SAUNDERS. Oh my God, this could be huge.

MARIA. What do you mean you want Racón?

TITO. Maria, you have betrayed me.

MARIA. "Betrayed you?"

TITO. I saw you with a man! *This* man! I saw you together!
I saw him pulling his clothing on!

MIMI. *(to* **CARLO***)* You see, it *is* the truth! It's the truth!

> (**MIMI** *slaps* **CARLO** *across the face again, sending
> him reeling across the room.*)

CARLO. Ow!!

MIMI. Get away from me! I hate you!

> (*Chaos erupts, everyone accusing everyone else.
> During the chaos,* **MAX** *– just like the wily servant
> in a Greek comedy – is putting everything together.*)

CARLO.	RACÓN.	SAUNDERS.	MIMI.	MARIA.	TITO.
I didn't do anything! What are you talking about?! I don't understand it!	*What is happening? Is being very confusing to me. I do not understand!*	*We have 15 minutes and we could lose the skinny conductor again!*	*(Through her tears.) You should be ashamed of yourself! How could you do such a thing!*	*Mimi, what is he do to you that is so terrible? How can you say that I betrayed you after all these years?*	*She's a-right! She's a-right! You have been sleeping with the man of my nightmares, Carlo Nucci.*

MAX. *STOP!!*

> *(The room falls silent.)*

Mimi, were you and Carlo fooling around in here this afternoon?

MIMI. Well –

CARLO. Yes, we were.

> *(to* TITO*)*

I'm sorry, sir.

TITO. Stay away from me!

MAX. And you left some clothes on the floor, didn't you.

MIMI. I guess we did.

MAX. Ha! Now Maria, did you tell Tito that you wanted Carlo to be one of the family?

MARIA. Yah. For Mimi. She is in love with him.

MAX. *(to* CARLO*)* And how did you get Maria's scarf?

CARLO. I don't know. I guess I took it without thinking.

MAX. Tito listen to me: Carlo is not Maria's lover. He wants to be your son-in-law.

MARIA. My "lover?"

TITO. Maria, is this true? You are not having affair with Carlo Nucci?

MARIA. Tito, he is half my age! Maybe it would not be so bad, but no! Of course not! Tito, we have been married for twenty-five years. I live for you. You are my life. How could you think such a thing?

(beat)

TITO. Because you are so beautiful, and so full of life. What man in the world would not want you for himself?

MARIA. That was the right answer.

(They kiss.)

MIMI. Oh, Carlo!

(They kiss.)

(RACÓN *throws herself against the bedroom door and sobs.*)

SAUNDERS. Excuse me, I'm very touched that you're all in love and I look forward to your exciting futures together, but *we have eight minutes until we start a concert in front of thirty thousand people!*

TITO. I will change to tux!

SAUNDERS. You mean you're doing the concert?

TITO. Of course I'm doing the concert!

(TITO *exits into the master bedroom.*)

SAUNDERS. Let's get the hell out on that stage!

(Everyone heads for the front door, babbling with excitement.)

MARIA. *Wait!* If that is Tito, then who is in there?

(MAX *and* SAUNDERS *look at each other.*)

MAX. I think we have to tell them, sir.

SAUNDERS. No.

MAX. Yes.

SAUNDERS. No.

MAX. Yes!

SAUNDERS. Oh all right!

MAX. His name is Beppo, and he's a bellhop here at the hotel.

RACÓN. *(aghast)* "Bellhop?"

MAX. Yeah.

(RACÓN sits.)

MAX. And he has this terrific voice and looks just like Tito.

MIMI. "Just like?" He's identical. He's Daddy's twin!

SAUNDERS. They say everybody in the world has a twin.

MAX. *(glancing at SAUNDERS)* That's sort of frightening.

RACÓN. *(knocking on the door, angry at the deception)* Beppo?

BEPPO. *(offstage)* Come in.

> *(She disappears into the room, leaving the door ajar. Everyone remaining onstage leans over, trying to see into the room.)*

SAUNDERS. You realize that we're down to seven minutes –

MARIA. Here he come.

> *(RACÓN and BEPPO come out of the bedroom.)*

BEPPO. *Ciao.*

> *(When the others see that he's identical to TITO, they gasp in wonder.)*

MARIA. I gave you my kiss.

MIMI. I gave you my heart.

RACÓN. I gave you my

> *(She gestures and makes a noise.)*

BEPPO. I'm a-sorry I have caused so much a-confusion, but that was not my intention, believe me. I just wanted to sing, that's all. But now of course Mr. Tito is back and you do not need me and I'm a-understand.

> *(He looks disappointed.)*

SAUNDERS. Well, we do have Tito now, and Carlo and Max. And Miss Racón, eh, hmm? Heh heh. So I'm afraid we do not in fact need your services this evening. Sorry, Beppo.

> *(BEPPO starts to leave.)*

MAX. If Beppo doesn't go on, I don't go on.

> *(beat)*

CARLO. Same here.

(*Beat. All eyes are on* **RACÓN**.)

RACÓN. (*to* **BEPPO**) "Bellhop." I am standing with Beppo, who is being my friend.

(*She takes his arm.*)

MAX. Mr. Saunders?

SAUNDERS. Oh, all right, he's in.

BEPPO. Ha-haaaaaaaaa!

SAUNDERS. Let's go, let's go! They're out there waiting!

(*Hubbub as they all head for the door.* **BEPPO** *is the first one out the door, and as he disappears, the rest start to follow:*)

BEPPO.	CARLO.	MAX.	RACÓN.	MARIA.	SAUNDERS.
I will sing my best tonight!	*I feel in such good voice, I just can't wait!*	*It's such an honor to sing with you.*	I will sing *Tosca* tonight, my favorite!	*Tito! Come! I fix your cuff link.*	Stop dallying, get a move on, let's go!

MIMI. (*touching her stomach*) I just hope all this excitement hasn't hurt the baby!

(*They all stop and look at her.*)

MARIA. Baby?

CARLO. Baby?

TITO. (*offstage*) Baby?!!

MIMI. I was waiting for the right moment to tell everybody. Isn't it great!

CARLO.	MARIA.	MAX.	RACÓN.
Oh, Mimi! I can't believe it! Oh my God!	My beautiful girl! I have been waiting so long for this!	Congratulations. I'm really happy for you.	This is being most wonderful event.

SAUNDERS. All right, all right! Congratulations, we're very touched, but we have six minutes to get on that stage! Max, are you ready?

MAX. Yes sir.

SAUNDERS. Carlo?

CARLO. Ready.

SAUNDERS. Miss Racón?

RACÓN. Da.

SAUNDERS. Tito? …Tito?

(*TITO hurries out of the bedroom in his tux.*)

TITO. Of course I'm a-ready, but the answer is a-NO! I will not go out on the stage with this boy! He has dishonored my family and they must a-be married first or I don't a-go!!

MIMI. Daddy!

MARIA. Tito!

CARLO. Mr. Merelli!

SAUNDERS. But we have less than six minutes left!

TITO. Then find a priest.

SAUNDERS. I don't know a priest!

TITO. That is your problem.

SAUNDERS. Jesus Christ.

MAX. He was a rabbi. Tito, listen. What about a civil ceremony with a priest later?

TITO. Is okay with me.

MAX. Sir, when you were Mayor of Cleveland you had the right to perform weddings.

TITO. He is no longer mayor.

MAX. But the right continues after leaving office. I remember the statute.

TITO. I don't believe you.

MAX. I have a good memory.

TITO. Max you are lying.

SAUNDERS. *For God's sake!*

MAX. (*Fast!*) Quote: "Powers to be retained by virtue of the Office of Mayor in perpetuity shall include: *one*, the power to attend City Council meetings; *two*, the power to represent the City on ceremonial occasions when the current Mayor is unable to attend; and *three*, the power *to perform civil marriages that shall be binding upon the participants thereto!*"

SAUNDERS. Kneel, my children.

> (**SAUNDERS** *puts out his hands in benediction, and everyone, together, kneels at the same time.*)

MAX. Who's the best man?

CARLO. Do you mind?

MAX. I'd love to.

MIMI. I need a bridesmaid.

RACÓN. I am having pleasure?

MIMI. Yes, please!

RACÓN. I am wanting the bouquet.

SAUNDERS. *May I begin?!*

MARIA. *(sniffling with emotion)* Yes, I am ready.

SAUNDERS. *(speaking quickly)* Dearly beloved we are gathered here in the sight of God to join these two in holy matrimony –

MAX. Sir, it's civil. Sight of "God"?

SAUNDERS. Dearly beloved we are gathered here in the sight of this soccer field to join these two in holy matrimony –

MAX. Actually "holy" matrimony means –

SAUNDERS. *SHUT UP!* Do you take this man to be your husband for better or worse, in sickness and health till death do you part?

MIMI. Yes!

SAUNDERS. Do you take this woman to be your wife for better or worse, in sickness and health till death do you part?

CARLO. Yes!

MIMI. What about the ring?!

> (**MARIA** *wrenches hers off her finger.*)

MARIA. Here, take this.

> (*Everyone except* **SAUNDERS** *huddles together to admire the ring.*)

RACÓN. Oh, is beautiful.

MAX. Wow, look at that.

TITO. Is a platinum setting.

MARIA. And they are real diamonds –

SAUNDERS. *Would you stop that!*

MIMI. Sorry.

CARLO. Sorry.

MARIA. Sorry.

MAX. Sorry.

SAUNDERS. *(defiantly)* Does anyone *object* to this marriage?!

MIMI & CARLO. *No!*

SAUNDERS. Bow your heads.

> *(They do.)*

By the power vested in me by the City of Cleveland and the concert we are about to perform I now pronounce you man and wife *now get the hell out of here! Go, go, go, go!*

> *(As everyone runs out the door, the lights change, a curtain comes in and suddenly we're backstage behind the curtain at the concert bowl of the Olympic Soccer Stadium. We hear the orchestra tuning up and we hear the hum of voices backstage and beyond the curtain.)*

> *(**MARIA** and **MIMI** run in first.)*

MIMI. *This is so exciting!*

MARIA. *You are married woman! My daughter is a-married!*

MIMI. *Eeeeeeeeee!*

MARIA. And Carlo is such a handsome boy. But I tell you, these opera singers they need a lot o' maintenance.

MIMI. Believe me, I know.

MARIA. Wait. Wait wait. I have an idea. I'll be right back.

> *(She runs off as **SAUNDERS** enters, calling into the wings.)*

SAUNDERS. *Come on, come on! We have to to start!*

(And now **MAX**, **RACÓN** *and* **CARLO** *hurry in and start adjusting their clothes and hair, doing voice exercises, etc.)*

MAX. Sir, the place is packed!

RACÓN. Mi mi mi mi mi –

CARLO. Ma ma ma ma ma –

MAX. Wooaa, wooaa, wooaa, wooaa –

SAUNDERS. *Where's Beppo?!*

RACÓN. Beppo?!

SAUNDERS. *Beppo?!!*

BEPPO. *(Hurrying on in his tux, wearing a red silk scarf.)* I'm a-here, I'm a-here!

(He looks around, taking it all in.)

I can feel it, this is a-my destiny. The crowds a do-not scare me at all, the lights a-warm me like my mama's smile, my heart a-sing, and I do this for Venezia, for the land of my people, for my father and for his father's a-father –

SAUNDERS. *SHUT UP!*

(Ring-ring! A backstage telephone rings.)

JACQUES. *(offstage) Meester Saunder, quick! Zere is a call coming through backstage! Someone please pick up!*

SAUNDERS. Now? Are you crazy? What are you talking about?!

JACQUES. *(offstage)* Max, is for you!

*(***MAX** *hurries to the edge of the stage and takes a receiver from an unseen hand. It has a long cord, so Max remains on stage.)*

MAX. Hello? *Maggie!!* Are you all right?! Oh my God, you're kidding.

(to the others)

I'm a father.

THE OTHERS. *(an explosion, giving* **MAX** *hugs and shaking his hand)* Hey, hey! / Oh, Max! / *Fantastico!*

MAX. Oh, Maggie, I'm so sorry I wasn't there to be with you. I love you so much.

SAUNDERS. *(grabs phone)* Maggie, it's Daddy! Good job! Keep it up!

MAX. *(grabs phone back)* Wait! Is it a boy or girl?

(to the others)

It's a boy.

(another cheer)

RACÓN. Oh, Beppo. Can I be havink one, too?

BEPPO. Oh we are gonna start tonight.

RACÓN. Heeheeeeee!

MAX. *(into the phone)* Henry, it's Daddy. Can you hear me? Henry?

SAUNDERS. You named him after me?

MAX. Yeah, we did.

SAUNDERS. Max.

(He slaps **MAX** *on the back.)*

MAX. Listen: can I wait to go on till the second half? I'd like to talk to Maggie for a while.

SAUNDERS. Of course, of course. Tell Maggie that I send my love. And Jacques, dear boy, would you be so kind as to announce the concert before I have a *heart attack!*

(The lights change and **JACQUES** *begins. We hear his voice reverberating over the arena's sound system. During the following,* **MAX** *continues talking to Maggie, but at first we can't hear him.)*

JACQUES. *Mesdames et messieurs. Bienvenue au Stade Olympique – welcome to ze Olympic Stadium of Paris for ze concert of ze century: Ze Four Tenors and ze Soprano!*

(We hear a roar from the stands.)

C'est mon honneur to introduce to you ze stars of ze show: Premier, si'l vous plait, please welcome a new but wonderful tenor from Venezia, Italy, un ténor known as BEPPO!

*(*RACÓN *gives* **BEPPO** *a kiss, and then he goes out onstage to nice applause.)*

JACQUES. *Et maintenant, alors, a young man who is one of ze best opera star in ze world today, please welcome CARLO NUCCI!*

> (**CARLO** *kisses* **MIMI**, *then strides out through the curtain and gets tumultuous applause.*)

And now we 'ave for you a fantastic surprise,

> (*As he speaks,* **MARIA** *does her pre-show backstage routine of pacing back and forth with her arms outstretched, concentrating deeply.*)

a soprano who is known from ze Met in New York to La Scala Milan, from St. Petersburg Russia, MISS TATIANA RACÓN!

> (**RACÓN** *throws her head back and walks onto the stage like the goddess she is and receives wild applause and cheers.*)

> (*At this point a drumroll is heard, announcing the biggest moment of the introduction. The audience is hushed. The moment has arrived.*)

SAUNDERS. *(looking around)* Wait! Jacques! Wait! Where the hell is Tito?!

MARIA. He was a-right behind me!

MIMI. I just saw him!

SAUNDERS. *TITO!!!*

> (**TITO** *runs in, smoothing his hair and adjusting his tux. He wears a white silk scarf.*)

TITO. I'm a-sorry! I'm a-sorry! There were girls at the stage door, four a-deep, they make a fuss, "Hey Tito, look this a-way," they want a-my picture, they were…

> (*Then it dawns on him…did* **MARIA** *arrange them? He points his finger at her with a questioning look.*)

Maria? Did you –?

> (*She shrugs as if to say: who knows. But of course she did arrange them, out of love for* **TITO**.)

MARIA. I guess you are still hot-stuff, eh?

(*TITO kisses* **MARIA** *with rapture as* **JACQUES** *continues.*)

JACQUES. (*drumroll*) *Et enfin, and finally ladies and gentlemen, ze star you 'ave been waiting for, ze most famous singer throughout ze world, please welcome TITO MERELLI!!*

(*TITO walks through the curtain and the crowd goes wild. The orchestra plays the introduction to "O Sole Mio," and we hear the four singers singing the song to the roaring crowd.*)

TITO, CARLO, RACÓN, BEPPO. (*offstage*)

MA N'ATU SOLE
CCHIÙ BELLO, OJE NE'.
O SOLE MIO
STA 'NFRONTE A TE!
O SOLE
O SOLE MIO
STA 'NFRONTE A TE!
STA 'NFRONTE A TE!

(*Meanwhile, a light picks out* **MAX**, *behind the curtain to one side, sitting on the floor, talking to Maggie.*)

MAX. No kidding. Wow, he's big. Yeah, I would like to talk to him again. Hello, Henry. Henry, it's Daddy.

(*And then the curtain opens behind* **MAX** *and we see all four singers from behind – including both* **TITO** *and* **BEPPO** *at the same time – swelling to the ending of the song, as the crowd goes wild.*)

(*The lights dim on the singers and then on* **MAX**, *his face glowing with happiness.*)

End of Play

(*The curtain call is a retelling of the whole play in 100 seconds to a cut-down version of the Verdi's overture to* Nabucco.)

REVISITING THE TENORS:
AN AFTERWORD FROM THE AUTHOR

Not long ago, I wrote a companion piece to my 1989 comedy *Lend Me A Tenor* and called it *A Comedy of Tenors*, and it recently received its world premiere in a co-production of the McCarter Theatre and the Cleveland Play House.

I have referred to the new play elsewhere as a "sequel," but I have to confess, I'm not fond of the word. In fact, the new play has turned out to be totally independent of the first, and the theatergoer does not need to know anything at all about *Lend Me A Tenor* in order to enjoy *A Comedy of Tenors*. They are their own plays set in their own worlds, and each play stands on its own.

Why then write a play at all using characters from the earlier play? I suppose because, over the years, I've become rather partial to the band of loonies in *Lend Me A Tenor* and I thought it might be instructive revisiting them lo these many years later. It has, in fact, proved to be a complete joy.

I never dreamed of writing the second play until four years ago when *Lend Me A Tenor* had a Broadway revival. As I sat in the audience, I could see how much the people around me enjoyed being in the company of my old friends from the Cleveland Grand Opera Company, and I was reminded how much I liked them myself. Then one night I had a thought:

"What if I wrote a play about these characters two years after the end of *Lend Me A Tenor*? Where would Max – dogsbody and aspiring opera star – be? Would he be singing for a living? Would Max and his girlfriend Maggie be married? What about the world famous opera star Tito Merelli and his wildcat wife Maria? Would they still be together?"

Typically, when I get an idea for a new play, I start thinking about how other playwrights have handled the same theme. In this case, I started thinking about the whole concept of a companion piece. Were there any really good ones back there in the history of drama?

Many of my favorite plays bear the distinctive marks of their comic creators. For example, Sheridan's 18th century *The School for Scandal* is clearly a kissing cousin of his early comic masterpiece *The Rivals*; but none of my favorite comedies fit the actual sequel category. *The Merry Wives of Windsor*? It contains several of the characters in *Henry IV, Parts 1 & 2*, but it's really more about Falstaff in love than a continuation of the histories.

In a way, the dearth of sequels in the theater is rather surprising. The urge to see our favorite characters for a second or third time is a natural one, and we see this urge satisfied time and again in movies, television and books. In the 1930s, the movie *The Thin Man* was an instant hit, and it was followed immediately by five more films about the same mystery-solving socialites. In television it's a commonplace. How many millions of us have loved following the Dowager Countess played by Maggie Smith in *Downton Abbey* over the years? Almost all of television is made up of sequels in this sense – they call 'em episodes. And don't forget all the books that have the same nucleus of characters, from Ian Fleming's James Bond thrillers to the Jeeves and Wooster series by P.G. Wodehouse. As Bertie Wooster would say, "Still with me? Right ho!"

So: loads of series and sequels and companion pieces in other art forms, almost none in the theatre. But there is one whopping exception and it was written by the stunningly-named Pierre-Augustin Caron de Beaumarchais. Beaumarchais wrote *The Barber of Seville* in 1773, then a few years later he wrote *The Marriage of Figaro* using four of the major characters from the earlier play and setting it three years later in time. Both plays are masterpieces, and they were both made into the best comic operas this side of paradise.

What's really interesting is that while *The Marriage of Figaro* is just as hilarious as *Barber,* it has a whole different tone. It asks some serious questions about marriage and politics, and it brings the lives of its characters full circle. These two plays encouraged me to forge ahead, and to try it in a similar way.

In writing *A Comedy of Tenors,* I started thinking about my life as a writer and how artists can have a hard time balancing the conflict between art and life. I have two monstrous things called children, a girl and a boy, and there are times when I'm in production for a new play, a continent away, sitting in a theater for days at a time, when I wonder how badly I'm short-changing the little creatures. This question set off a few bells as I scribbled my way through *A Comedy of Tenors.*

In the play, superstar Tito Merelli has been married for twenty-five years, all the while spending weeks at a time performing on the road. How does his wildly demonstrative wife Maria put up with it? And how has it affected his glamorous young actress daughter Mimi? Will Mimi end up marrying a fellow artist herself? And if so, will that put her in conflict with her artist father? Exploring these characters a bit more deeply this time around, while keeping them buoyant and funny (oh Lord, I hope so) felt like exactly the right place to be.

It was clear to me from the minute I put pen to paper (and I really do use a pen and paper) that I wanted the form of the play to be a traditional farce. This was the form I used in *Lend Me A Tenor* and it felt equally appropriate here since I was still dealing with extravagant characters in a glamorous setting.

I was very aware that by choosing a specific theatrical form, I was setting up certain expectations, and I welcomed them. When you write a farce, you play by certain rules, one of which is to keep the plot as light as air while delivering as much wit and wisdom along the way as you can muster. In a tragedy of the Shakespearean variety, someone noble dies at the end. That's the convention; it's not debatable. In a traditional farce, it is equally non-debatable that there will be mistaken identity, romantic couples (usually two or three), a sense of buoyant sexiness, and loads of word play.

I have seen farce criticized for being "lowbrow," but of course that's missing the point entirely. The great Shakespearean critic Northrop Frye likens the situation to that of a doctor friend who saw *Twelfth Night* and couldn't bear it because he knew that it was biologically impossible for boy-girl twins to be identical. Frye's response is that you simply have to accept Shakespeare's conventions at face value in order to enjoy the plays. There is no in-between. As Shakespeare himself puts it in *The Winter's Tale*, "It is required/You do awake your faith."

My own favorite authors in the world of farce include the late-19th Century Frenchman Georges Feydeau, whose masterpieces include *A Flea in her Ear* and *The Lady from Maxim's*; his slightly older near-contemporary, Eugene Labiche, who famously wrote *The Italian Straw Hat, Pots of Money* and dozens of other plays; the aforementioned genius Beaumarchais and his Figaro plays; Sir Arthur Wing Pinero, the first playwright in history to be knighted and the author of *The Magistrate and Dandy Dick*; and Ben Travers, who wrote a series of farces for the Whitehall Theatre in London in the early 20th century.

If I expand this list to include comedies with farcical moments in them, I would then be adding my favorite comedies of all time: Shakespeare's *Midsummer, Taming of the Shrew, Much Ado, Twelfth Night* and *As You Like It*; Oliver Goldsmith's *She Stoops to Conquer*; Sheridan's *The Rivals* and *The School for Scandal*; John O'Keeffe's *Wild Oats*; Oscar Wilde's *The Importance of Being Earnest*; Bernard Shaw's *Arms and the Man*; Noel Coward's *Private Lives*; and Kaufman and Hart's *The Man Who Came to Dinner*.

As I applied these thoughts and recollections to *A Comedy of Tenors*, the immediate question was the plot. (Farces are relentlessly plot-driven.) In this case, the plot came surprisingly quickly, partly because I based it on an historical event:

In 1990, a music producer came up with a pretty wild idea. He would stage a charity concert starring the three greatest tenors in the world – Luciano Pavarotti, Placido Domingo and José Carreras – and he would present it at the Baths of Caracalla in Rome on the eve of the World Cup soccer finals. He called it "The Three Tenors," and it turned out to be the classical concert of the century. To this day, the album is the best-selling classical album of all time, and the follow-up concert (the sequel, if you will) was watched by over 1.3 billion viewers on international television.

So my premise was this: Henry Saunders, the wily producer of the Cleveland Grand Opera Company from *Lend Me A Tenor*, has come up with the same idea, only fifty years earlier, in 1936. He's staging a concert in Paris called "The Three Tenors" starring Max, Tito and Jussi Björling – and he's doing it at a soccer stadium which happens to be located next to one of the finest hotels in Paris, where the action of the play unfolds.

After that, the plot was simplicity itself: Tito is having a mid-life crisis. Max and Maggie are having a baby. The famous Russian soprano Tatiana Racón, who is Tito's former lover, is visiting Paris. Tito and Maria's daughter, Mimi, is also in town with her own lover. And everything that possibly could go wrong does go wrong.

The writing of *A Comedy of Tenors* has turned out to be more fulfilling than I'd ever imagined. I thought I had said goodbye to the characters in *Lend Me A Tenor* when the play first opened on Broadway so many years ago, but *A Comedy of Tenors* has not only been a joy to write and produce from beginning to end, it has also allowed me to spend time once again with some of my best friends in the world.

Ken Ludwig

February 2016

KEN LUDWIG has had six shows on Broadway and seven in London's West End, and his plays and musicals have been performed in more than 30 countries in over twenty languages. His first play on Broadway, *Lend Me A Tenor,* which the *Washington Post* called "one of the classic comedies of the 20th century," won two Tony Awards and was nominated for seven. He has also won two Laurence Olivier Awards (England's highest theater honor), the Charles MacArthur Award, two Helen Hayes Awards, the Edgar Award for Best Mystery from The Mystery Writers of America, the SETC Distinguished Career Award, and the Edwin Forrest Award for Services to the American Theatre. His plays have been commissioned by the Royal Shakespeare Company and the Bristol Old Vic. He has written 23 plays and musicals, including *Crazy For You* (five years on Broadway and the West End, Tony and Olivier Award Winner for Best Musical), *Moon Over Buffalo* (Broadway and West End), *The Adventures of Tom Sawyer* (Broadway), *Treasure Island* (West End), *Twentieth Century* (Broadway), *Baskerville, Leading Ladies, Shakespeare in Hollywood, The Game's Afoot, The Fox on the Fairway, The Three Musketeers* and *The Beaux' Stratagem.* His play *A Comedy of Tenors* was chosen to mark the 100th Anniversary of the Cleveland Playhouse and was co-produced by the McCarter Theatre. His newest book, *How To Teach Your Children Shakespeare,* won The Falstaff Award for Best Shakespeare Book of 2014 and is published by Random House. His plays have starred Alec Baldwin, Carol Burnett, Lynn Redgrave, Mickey Rooney, Hal Holbrook, Dixie Carter, Tony Shalhoub, Anne Heche, Joan Collins, and Kristin Bell. His work is published by the Yale Review, and he is a Sallie B. Goodman Fellow of the McCarter Theatre. He holds degrees from Harvard, where he studied music with Leonard Bernstein, Haverford College and Cambridge University. For more information, please visit www.kenludwig.com.